Mr. Nobody

By Natalie Gordon

For Millie and Isla

Mr. Nobody

By Natalie Gordon

Contents

Mum and Dad tell us "The News"

Katie

"Katie! Are you listening to me?"

I stopped eating and looked at Mum. I hadn't heard, because I'd been thinking about school today. Carys had been all mean again and Anna had joined in, so me and Molly hid by the bushes for the whole of lunch break. It was kind of nice in the end, especially when Molly started doing impressions of the teachers. She pretended to be Mrs. Jackson with a Scooby Doo voice and we couldn't stop laughing, but then Carys found us and thought we were laughing at her and she went off in a strop. She was always going off in a strop. It was really annoying.

"I said, I have some news."

Mum looked stressed and Lou was giving

me her Look, the one where she puts her head to one side and smirks. She was always giving me or Mum and Dad a Look. She used to be fun, but not any more: too busy flicking her hair around or texting her boyfriend, Max. I didn't want to be a teenager.

"Your gran is coming to stay with us for a bit."

Lou stopped smirking at me and stared at Mum, like she'd said something nasty to us.

"You mean *your* mum?"

"Yes."

"Oh, great."

Lou pulled a face. She didn't get on with Mum's mum. Gran seemed to have the knack of saying stuff that annoyed Lou. Maybe that was why I liked her.

"I'm picking her up at the weekend. She's going to live with us for a while."

"Why? Is she ill, Mum?"

"Yes, Katie, she is kind of ill."

"What's wrong with her?"

"It's just old age. She can't look after herself properly any more."

So she wasn't really ill then, just old. But old people get older, so she wasn't going to get any better at looking after herself, was she? Lou must have been thinking the same as me. Sometimes, I like having an older sister to ask the questions I don't dare ask. Just sometimes, though.

"Well, if she's coming because she's old, she's never going to go home again, is she? Why do *we* have to have her? Why can't Aunty Sal look after her?"

"Lou!"

That was in Dad's teacher voice, with a proper teacher stare to go with it. If I didn't know him, and if he were my teacher, I'd be scared of him. Lou hated that he taught at her school. I didn't think Dad could like it much either, though – it can't be fun if other teachers come and tell you how annoying your daughter is all the time.

"Aunty Sal can't look after her – she has enough on her plate with the twins. She's my mother, she needs help and I'm not going to abandon her hundreds of miles away to fend for herself."

She's Aunty Sal's mum too, but I guess Mum is better at looking after her because she's a nurse.

"You don't have to *abandon* her."

The way Lou said the word 'abandon' made me hold my breath in case she said "stupid" at the end. She sounded just like she did when she was about to say something mean to me, but I guess she wasn't quite brave enough to talk to Mum like that. I let my breath out again slowly as she carried on.

"I just meant, well, it doesn't have to be us, does it? And anyway we haven't got a room for her. Where are you going to put her?"

Dad reached over and took Mum's hand and squeezed it without looking at her. He was looking at Lou and he looked annoyed.

"Firstly, we're not *putting* her anywhere. She's coming to stay with us. Secondly, this isn't a negotiation. We are going to help your gran because she's family and because your mother and I thought that you two would be old enough and mature enough to understand that we have to do this. We were obviously wrong about that."

"Yeah, obviously."

Lou slumped back in her chair and crossed her arms in front of her, looking with her Evil Eyes at Mum and Dad.

Dad ignored her and turned to me.

"Katie, you're unusually quiet?"

I shrugged. I didn't know what to say. I didn't really understand what all the fuss was about or why it felt like they were saying things, but not saying the important things.

Lou was still giving them her Evil Look when she asked, "So how long *is* she going to stay with us, then?"

It was Mum's turn to answer now. She sounded tired.

"We don't know. She probably won't go back to her own house again."

"I don't get it. Why didn't you tell us before? I mean, yesterday there was nothing wrong with her, and today she's so incapable of looking after herself you're going to get her at the weekend. Why's it so sudden?"

Lou didn't sound cross now, more kind of sulky, but it was a good question. I felt like a ball girl watching a tennis match. Any minute now one side would hit the ball in the net and I would have to jump up to rescue it.

"We didn't tell you before, because we didn't think there was anything to say, but it seems that Gran's got worse in the last few weeks and really needs to be somewhere we can keep an eye on her."

They still hadn't explained where she was going to sleep. We didn't have a spare room, not like Carys who had a spare room and a playroom and a conservatory, even though she didn't have any brothers or sisters. We had an average kind of house, bigger than Molly's, but the same as Anna's because she lived on the same road. Lou looked at Mum and asked the question in my head.

"So, where's Gran going to sleep?"

"Well, it's not forever, but you two will have to share. Katie, you'll move into Lou's room."

Mum stopped and looked at us. I didn't know what Lou's face looked like at that moment because I couldn't seem to take my eyes off Mum's mouth where those words had just come out. I was willing them to go back into her mouth somehow, like when you rewind a DVD. She couldn't have meant it.

"I know it's not ideal, but there is no other way."

I couldn't speak. Lou screamed at Mum.

"There is no way that I am *ever* sharing my room with *her*."

She jabbed her finger at me and jumped up from the table, knocking her chair over as she did so.

"There's no way. Why can't Gran go into an old people's home or something? It's not happening. You can't do this!"

I wished for once that they would listen to her, because I couldn't see how I could possibly share a room with Lou. I felt sick at the thought of it. I liked my own space. My room was perfect. I loved it. It was all green and white apart from the orange shooting stars on my duvet cover. I had everything just where I wanted it. There was my desk where I did my drawings, with the art set I got for Christmas, which had loads of different pencils and pens and highlighters and opened out into three different levels. I had my picture frames all around my walls with all my own art in them, my squishy turquoise beanbag next to my bookcase where I would curl up for hours with a book if I could, and my bed with the cuddly toys I'd had since I was little. It wouldn't all fit in Lou's room. I started to cry.

"Look at her. She's a baby. I'm *not* sharing with her."

Lou stormed out of the room.

"You come back down here and apologise to your sister. It's not all about you."

He was wrong. It *was* all about Lou. It was always all about her. I knew that better than Dad did. I was really crying now. Mum came over and hugged me into her chest. I let her, but secretly I was mad with her. I buried my head in her fleecy jumper and cried some more. I felt hot and angry and upset and mad and scared, all mixed up and ready to burst like Mr. Braithwaite's volcano experiment. Worst of all I felt like someone somewhere had taken a rubber and started to ever so slowly rub a little bit of me away.

2

My room isn't mine any more

Katie

It was Saturday.

Saturday was The Day. I was moving out and Gran was moving in.

I liked Gran. We didn't see her much because she lived so far away, but when we did see her, she and I got on. We found the same random things funny and we liked making cakes. We liked eating them too and I always got to lick the bowl out. If it hadn't been for giving her my room, I would have been more excited about seeing her.

Dad had to wake Lou up. He and I were ready. He was extra chatty, I wasn't. I'd got up early and carefully arranged the things I was going to put away into one pile and the things I was keeping in the other pile. There wasn't room for all my stuff in Lou's room, so I had to pack some things away. It wasn't fair. It was like I was being cleared away to make room for Gran: no one would have dared to clear Lou away.

If I didn't have all my stuff, and I didn't have my room any more, it was like it wasn't my home, and that was like I didn't really belong in my own family. Actually, it's like when you roll out the pastry to make a pie, there's always a bit left over that you don't know what to do with.

It was too hard to explain to Dad that I felt like a bit of leftover pastry. He wouldn't get it, so I kept moving things from one pile to the other, trying to decide what to pack away and what to keep. The cuddlies were the hardest. Should I take all of them, or should I just take a few? I decided to just take the ones that still lived on my bed: Rabbit and Owly and Ted and also Pinky and Floppy. I felt bad about the rest. I couldn't look at them so I covered them over with some old dressing up clothes before I changed my mind.

Dad came in with some boxes, but before he did any packing he came over and we had a really long, squeezy hug. I didn't want it to end. I wanted him to stay and say he was sorry and it was all a silly mistake, but he didn't. Instead, we packed my things away together; we had a snack just like proper removal men and then we were ready to tackle The Room, but Lou hadn't come out of it yet. Dad went up to sort her out. I stayed in the kitchen and looked out of the window, but I wasn't in the mood for waving at the postman today.

I heard Dad knock on her door and then open it and shut it behind him. Normally I might have crept up the stairs to listen in, but not today. It took Dad a while. She only shouted twice though, so whatever Dad was saying to her must have worked. Then I heard her stamp down the stairs. She stormed into the kitchen and glared at me. I ignored her and edged past her to go upstairs, but she just couldn't resist it, could she?

"Don't you DARE touch any of my stuff!"

I didn't want her stupid stuff, but if she was going to be mean about it then I might just feel like moving some of it. I ignored her again because she hated that.

"Did you HEAR ME, you stupid cow?"

She yelled the first bit like I was deaf, but she said the second bit really quietly so Dad wouldn't hear. I smiled like I didn't care what she said and I didn't answer her. Stupid cow herself.

"LOU! Stop that now!"

Dad was at the top of the stairs leaning over the banisters looking hot and grumpy. I think he'd been moving furniture.

"I don't want any more of that kind of talk. Lou stay out of the way and Katie come up here and help, will you?"

That was unfair. I hadn't done anything. He should just be shouting at Lou. I opened my mouth to tell him that, but shut it again when I saw his eyes. They were the big scary popping out eyes that he got when he was really cross. I reached the top landing. He was sweating so I didn't get too close. I didn't want him to know that I'd noticed the little raindrops of sweat running down the side of his face, in case he got embarrassed.

"Right, I've made some space so all you need to do is get your stuff up here while I bring the little bookcase up."

"OK, Dad."

I peered past him into her room and saw that he had put the pullout bed on the other side of the room to Lou's bed. Good, I didn't want to be near her. Gran was having my bed. Lou had said that Gran might wet the bed, but I didn't believe her.

While I was arranging my books and art stuff on the shelves of my new bookcase, Lou came in. Dad was downstairs having a cup of tea before he started making my room into Gran's room. I didn't look at her, but I knew she was looking at me. I carried on with what I was

11

doing, but I wished she would go away, because I needed to find a good hiding place for my special pictures. I also wanted to choose some of my best pictures to put on my pin board that Dad had put next to the bed.

"You do know this won't be forever, don't you?"

Lou's voice was funny, like she was trying to speak in a mean voice but couldn't quite manage it. I looked at her. She was sitting on her bed twisting her long dark hair between her fingers and just staring at me. People said we looked the same, but it was just our hair. I stared back. I couldn't work out what mood she was in, so I didn't say anything.

"I mean, Gran's not going to get better so you know what that means, don't you?"

I shrugged. Sometimes it's best not to say anything.

Lou stopped fiddling with her hair and leant forward.

"It means that you'll get your room back when she's dead."

She lowered her voice.

"And when they've taken her body away you can have your bed back."

Her top lip curled up as she whispered, "In the room of death."

She was saying what was inside my head. I

hated her for it. It made it real.

"I HATE YOU! I'm telling Dad what you said. You're HORRIBLE!"

"I'm telling Dad what you said."

She mimicked me in her stupid false high voice that didn't sound anything like me.

"Go on then. See if I care. I'm going out. If you touch anything of mine I'll rip up all your stupid pictures and don't think I won't. I mean it."

She snatched up her bag and thumped down the stairs. She and Dad shouted at each other and then she went out, banging the front door shut behind her. Dad hated it when she did that, which was probably why she did it.

I didn't want to stay up there after that. It also felt like The Room wanted me out, so I went downstairs and had lunch with Dad. We didn't say much, but sometimes that's OK. Some people don't like silence, but Dad and I didn't mind. Anyway he was tired and I didn't have any words left to use, because they were all jumbled up inside my head and kept bumping into Lou's death words. I felt like I needed to shake my head and let them all tip out, but Dad looked at me strangely when I tried it. Didn't work anyway.

After lunch, Dad's friend Dave came round with his van and he and Dad unloaded an old person's armchair, a small table and a telly. They carried them upstairs and moved the furniture around in my room to make it all fit.

I liked Dave. He could make coins appear behind your ear and he let you keep them. I was a bit too old for that trick now, but I wasn't stupid. I kept £3. After he'd gone I helped Dad to make the room look nice. It was like if it didn't look like my room, then maybe it wouldn't feel like my room.

Gran didn't like duvets so we put a sheet and blankets on the bed. They looked a bit scratchy to me but Dad said that's how she liked it. The old person's armchair was in the corner. It had those white lacy things on the arms and over the back. Dad said it was to stop greasy hair and sweaty hands leaving marks on the chair. I thought that was disgusting. I didn't think we'd have to protect the furniture and I really hoped we weren't going to do the same to the chairs downstairs. I didn't want to have to explain that to my friends.

We put the little telly on a small table in front of her armchair. I wondered if I could keep the telly when she died. We weren't allowed tellies in our rooms. I knew because Lou asked every Christmas for one and Dad said no, she could choose whichever books she wanted instead. I think that's why she hardly ever reads. Sometimes Dad says some really stupid teacher things like he thinks he's being clever, but Lou's pretty clever too.

My desk became part dressing table and part writing table. Dad had found a little mirror and I got some paper and envelopes and put them on the other half of the table. I knew Gran liked to write letters and cards. She'd once shown me a drawer stacked with postcards and letters she'd kept, some of them on that funny blue paper that she said people used to write on when they lived abroad. It crinkled like baking paper. I didn't know anyone who wrote letters apart from Gran. The only letters I ever wrote were thank you cards and they weren't very long.

By the middle of the afternoon we were tired out. Lou came back from town, without Max for a change. I was ready for a fight, but she wasn't in that kind of mood any more.

So by ten past three, when Mum and Gran arrived, the three of us were sitting silently at the kitchen table, munching through a pack of chocolate digestives. We were allowed more than two each. It really wasn't a normal day.

3

Vera gets ready to move into Katie's room

Vera (Gran)

Vera sat on her sofa and watched as Lisa packed another box. So much packing and unpacking and moving things around and taking things away. She didn't like it. She'd heard Lisa on the phone this morning, chatting to that husband of hers. Her son-in-law. What was his name? She never had liked him. Eyes too wide apart, and always too sure of himself. Pete used to like him, though. Her darling Pete. She missed him. He wouldn't put up with this, if he were still around. She was going to do something about it.

"Lisa, I want you to stop."

"I'm nearly done, Mum. I just want to get these things packed up. Jim from next door said he'd take them down to the charity shop for us."

"Well I don't see why. There's nothing wrong with those clothes."

"Mum, we've been through this. You have so many clothes that you never wear any more. We haven't got room for them at ours and if we leave them here, the moths will get them and we'll have to clear them out later anyway. Might as well do it now, while we're both here."

"There's really no need. I'm not going anywhere and nor are they."

"Mum, you're coming to live with Gary and me for a bit. Remember? You're going to stay in Katie's room and she's going to share Lou's room."

Vera frowned. She couldn't remember the conversation. She wished she could put her finger on what it was that was making her uneasy. Blasted old age.

"Oh. Well that seems like a lot of bother. There's really no need."

"It's fine, Mum. They're looking forward to seeing you again."

"Who are?"

"The girls: Katie and Lou."

"Will they be here soon?"

"No, Mum. As I've just said, I'm taking you to our home. They're waiting there for us."

"Oh, I see."

Vera sat and watched as Lisa took the box

out to the driveway. She didn't really see. It felt like a lot of fuss about nothing. She felt exhausted just watching Lisa bustling around, like she owned this house. She was sure she hadn't asked her to come round. And where was Katie? And Lou? She could swear Lisa had mentioned them just a moment ago. They'd be hungry, wouldn't they? She'd best go and start making some supper for them all. She got up and went into the kitchen and started to get a few things out of the fridge.

"Mum? What are you doing?"

"I'm getting supper ready for everyone, of course. What does it look like I'm doing?"

"Mum, it's only 10 o'clock in the morning and there's only you and me here. I've already told you: Katie and Lou and Gary are all waiting for you at home. My home. I'm driving you there today. Tell you what, shall we just have a cuppa before we go?"

"Well that's exactly what I was going to do. How many cups do we need?"

4

Gran moves in

Katie

We heard the squeak of the garden gate first. Lou and I looked at each other and Dad got up and opened the door. Gran stood there, Mum close behind her.

"There we go, Mum, safe and sound. In you go now."

"Hello, Vera. Good journey? Come on in."

I got up from the table and waited. Mum and Dad had put on false happy voices. I wasn't going to speak like that. She was just old, not stupid.

"Hi, Gran."

She looked at me and then she smiled and practically pushed Dad aside to come in and give me a hug. I let her squeeze me. She smelt like stale roses, which wasn't too bad really. And actually I loved Gran and hadn't seen her for months so it was nice to see her again, even if she did ruffle my hair.

"Oh look at you, haven't you grown? My little Lou, all grown up."

It was the matching hair again. Maybe I'd get mine cut.

"No Gran, I'm Katie. That's Lou."

Lou gave her a teenager smile that only stayed on for a few seconds, and she didn't bother getting up to give Gran a hug. Gran stared at her then grinned at me.

"Of course you're Katie! Silly me, getting it wrong again."

"That's OK, Gran. Do you want to see your room?"

"Oh Katie, it's been a long journey. Why don't you just let Gran sit down and rest? We'll have a cup of tea. Just let us get these bags in."

Mum sounded cross, but I was only trying to help and even Gran could see that.

"Lisa, don't fuss so. I've been sitting down all the way here. Now where did I put them?"

Gran was heading into the lounge like she was looking for something. I glanced at Mum, thinking she'd be cross with Gran for snapping at her like that, but she can't have heard her. I followed Gran into the lounge.

"What are you looking for, Gran?"

"My glasses. I'm sure I put them down in

here somewhere."

"You can't have done. You've only just got here."

Gran shook her head and ignored me. She started to poke around in the piles of stuff on the sofa. I was supposed to have tidied that up today.

"Come on, Gran, let's go back to the kitchen and have a cup of tea."

I didn't want Mum coming in and seeing I hadn't tidied up. That was my Saturday job.

"Katie, what did I say about settling Gran down with a cup of tea?"

It wasn't my fault. Was I supposed to stop Gran moving around?

"Granny was in the kitchen,
doing a bit of stitching,
when in came a bogie man
and pushed her out."

She'd sung it really quietly, so only I heard her and she must have known I'd heard, because she grinned at me and put her finger to her lips. She followed me back into the kitchen where Dad was glaring at Lou and Mum was putting the kettle on. Gran didn't normally sing random bits of song. At least, not that I remembered. Though she *was* an Elvis fan. We'd bought her a CD of his best hits for Christmas. She was humming something now and Lou was raising her eyebrows at me, trying to get me to laugh at Gran, I suppose. I frowned back at her.

"Ooh chocolate biscuits, they look nice. I'll just have one now, find the ladies room and be on my way."

Gran hadn't sat down yet and she was reaching out for one of the biscuits we'd been eating earlier. No one told her off, so I reached out for one as well.

"Katie! Manners! Sit down first and ask before you take one."

Gran was already making crumbs down her top. Lou smirked at me. That really wasn't fair.

"But, I…"

"No buts. Go and remind Gran where the toilet is, will you? Make yourself useful."

"And Lou, help your dad take Gran's bags up please, instead of just sitting there. Come on, both of you; shake a leg."

I was already being 10 times more helpful than Lou. There was no need for Mum to snap at me, but I didn't argue; I just glared. Lou wasn't the only one who could do Looks. No one saw me.

"Come on, Gran. The toilet's this way."

"Oh thank you, dear."

Gran caught hold of my arm and whispered, "Lisa was always the bossy one you know, don't you worry about her. She's got far too big for her boots since she married that man."

I thought that was a weird way to talk about Mum and Dad but I smiled anyway, left her at the loo and then ran up the stairs to my – Gran's – bedroom. Already, it didn't look at all like my room any more. Dad was in it, unpacking Gran's bags. I stood watching for a bit. He had just put a photo of Granddad Pete on the table when he looked up and saw me.

"OK, Katie?"

I half smiled and shrugged.

"It won't be for ever, you know."

"I know."

I didn't add, "I know because Lou said she'll die in my bed and then I can have my room back."

There wasn't any point. It would only wind Dad up and actually I didn't want to think about Gran dying. I'd kind of forgotten how much I liked her, because I'd been all caught up in the room stuff. But still, I really, really wanted my room. Then we heard Gran's voice.

"Now then, I don't know who you think you are, but will you kindly show me the way out."

Dad and I looked at each other. Gran was acting really weird.

"But Gran, you've only just got here, we're not going out anywhere."

"Mum, come on, let's go and look at your room shall we?"

My room.

They came upstairs, a Gran sandwich with Mum leading the way, Gran in the middle muttering something under her breath and Lou behind, actually looking like she didn't know how to look. That made a change. I moved back onto the landing, as my room wasn't very big. Mum took Gran's hand and led her into my bedroom. Lou stayed at the top of the stairs, fiddling with the ends of her hair. She wanted to dye the ends but Mum wouldn't let her. Lou said she was saving up and then she'd go and do it. We all ignored her, but I knew she would.

"Here you are, Vera. It's lovely, isn't it?"

Gran didn't look like she agreed with Dad. She probably missed her own room. I could understand that.

"Very nice but I really must be on my way now. Lisa, we must be off now, mustn't we?"

"No, Mum let's just unpack your bags first, shall we? See, Gary's already started."

We all waited. I'm not sure why but it seemed like we should, like we didn't know what Gran would do.

Then I think Gran must have spotted her knickers in the bag and not wanted Dad to touch them, because she pushed him out of the way and pulled them out. She sat on the bed, scrunching them up as small as she could, which wasn't very small because Gran was pretty fat. In a cuddly kind of way, not like a really fat unhealthy way, though she did eat a lot of cake.

> "Nellie Murphy's got no drawers.
> Won't you kindly lend her yours?
> For she's going far away
> to sing ta ra ra boom de ay."

That did it. Both Lou and I cracked up, but Gran wasn't laughing, she looked like she wanted to cry. Mum started trying to shoo me and Lou out of the way.

"Come on girls, why don't you leave us to it? Dad and I will get Gran settled."

Gran was sitting on my bed, rubbing her hands and turning her rings over and over. She'd stuffed the knickers under her pillow. Mum shut the door.

"Well, I'm glad *my* room isn't being used as a mental home. See you later, sis. Don't come up."

Then Lou ran upstairs and slammed her door. She never called me 'sis'. So here I was on the landing without a room and without a name.

5

I'm in charge

Katie

It was just me and Gran in the house.

She'd been with us for two weeks and this was the first time we'd been left alone in the house together. Mum was shopping, Lou was in town with Max, and Dad was doing something at the school, though when he'd told Mum this morning that he had to go to school, she wasn't happy.

So I was in charge, because Gran couldn't really look after me. She forgot everything. You could have the same conversation with her all day and she would never remember that we'd already talked about it. Lou said she couldn't be bothered to repeat herself all day, but Lou rude like that. Gran and I got on. Sometimes after school, I went up to her/my room and we listened to Elvis together. You didn't have to talk

26

then; you could just listen.

I decided that this morning we should bake a cake, because I know how to do it myself now. Gran could help and I knew she loved cake.

"Gran, I'll just get everything ready and then we can start."

"OK, my love. What are we making?"

"Chocolate sponge cake and we can make the icing out of melted chocolate. That's my favourite bit."

"Sounds delicious, dear."

I got out all the ingredients and the mixing bowl and stuff because it wasn't fair to ask Gran to get them out since it wasn't her kitchen, but while I was doing that, she went off somewhere. Probably to the loo. I started weighing out the chocolate, ready to put in the microwave to melt, like Mum had shown me.

The front door slammed which was odd, because it was too early for anyone to come home, unless they had forgotten something. I called out,

"Hello?"

There was no reply, so I shoved the dish into the microwave and set the timer before peering round the corner to see who it was, when Gran walked past the kitchen window. I hit the stop button on the microwave, ran to the door and flung it open, yelling,

"Gran! Where are you going?"

She didn't even turn around. I couldn't leave the house because I didn't have the keys with me – they were in the bowl in the kitchen. Mum had said to keep an eye on her, but she was a grown-up so she can't have meant I had to keep her inside. Could she? And then I saw that she still had her slippers on. I put the door on the latch and ran after her, praying that no one would come home and wonder why I hadn't locked up.

"Gran! Wait! Wait for me!"

I caught up with her and put my hand on her arm to stop her. She turned to me and looked startled, like I'd scared her. She must have been going deaf, because she should have heard me yelling.

"Gran, don't you want to make the cake?"

She frowned at me, like I was talking nonsense.

"Gran, we were making a cake, remember?"

"Hey, Katie, what are you doing?"

Oh no. I hadn't seen Carys and Anna on the other side of the road, just outside Anna's house. They had their arms linked together like they were best friends and they were laughing. At me. Gran waved at them, which made them laugh even more. Even worse, they started crossing the road.

"Gran, let's go home. Come *on*."

"I think they want to talk to you, Lou."

"No, Gran, I'm Katie. Come on, let's go."

I started to tug on Gran's arm, but she was ignoring me. I then realised that I was still wearing my apron and worse than that, I was in my slippers too. I took Gran's hand, just as Carys and Anna came up to us. I tried to pull her with me without making it obvious but Gran was standing there, smiling stupidly at my worst enemy.

"Hello. Are you Katie's gran?"

Carys smiled at Gran and then at me, but it wasn't a nice smile, it was a sneering smile and Anna just giggled and rolled her eyes. I hated her.

"Yes love, and are you her school friends?"

"Yep. She's told us all about you moving in. She's been SO looking forward to it."

I didn't want to be here any more. I started to drag Gran by the hand.

"Katie, don't be so rude."

"Gran, we need to go. We're baking a cake, remember?"

"Oh well, I'm sure it can wait."

"Oh don't worry about us, we're going into town anyway. Is that where you were going in your slippers?"

They started laughing and trying (not very hard) to hide it behind their hands. I could feel my face burning.

"Just shut up, will you?"

I didn't say it loudly because I didn't want Gran to hear and do something embarrassing, like tell me off in front of them. I shouldn't have been worried though, because I don't think Gran had heard me. She was looking down at her feet. I really wished I hadn't been left in charge. Carys and Anna started to go down the hill, looking over their shoulders and laughing. Since when had *they* become best friends?

Gran was ready to come with me now. We walked home without speaking. I was mad with her for embarrassing me, mad with Carys for being so rude to Gran and mad with Anna for not being my friend any more and mad with Mum and Dad *and* Lou for just leaving me at home this morning. I was so busy being mad with everyone, that I didn't see the old lady coming towards us until I nearly tripped over her dog; a black Labrador. I LOVE black Labradors.

"Hugo, come on, out of the way."

The old lady smiled at me apologetically, glanced at Gran and tried to pull her dog past us. He was so cute, I stopped being mad and bent down to stroke his ears, but he tried to hide behind the old lady's legs. Mum and Dad won't let me have a dog. They said if I really want a pet, I can have a guinea pig, but guinea pigs are stupid; they just sit there all day. And they smell.

I know because Anna has two.

"He's too bouncy for his own good. We're just going up to the woods to work off some of that energy. Aren't we, Hugo?"

He didn't look very bouncy. He had big sad eyes, that were staring at me as if he was trying to work me out. I tried to coax him out from the old lady's legs and he came and sniffed my hand. I looked up at the old lady and she grinned at me. She seemed nice and she was wearing awesome trousers. They were funky purple combats. I looked from her to Gran: same height, same age I guessed, but this old woman just seemed younger and more kind of, well, with-it, though not very gran-like.

Gran was backing away from the dog, though I don't know why, because he seemed more scared of her. I couldn't help thinking it, but I did wonder just then what my morning might have been like if I could have swapped them over and made the woman with the dog my gran. I bet I wouldn't have met Carys and Anna in my slippers and apron on the pavement and, if we had seen them, I bet she would have realised that we needed to get inside fast. I stood up and smiled at the old lady, then turned to Gran.

"Come on, Gran, let's go."

"Lovely to meet you."

Weird. Gran did that sometimes, being all

friendly to people she didn't know. Sometimes I thought she was nicer to strangers than she was to Mum. I didn't have time to think about that though, because I could see Lou coming up the hill.

I pulled on Gran's hand and got us inside just before Lou. Something was very wrong.

"Katie, what *are* you doing? And *what* is that smell?"

I rushed into the kitchen. It stank of burning. I felt my stomach literally in my mouth. The microwave. I opened it and started to cough as the smoke hit the back of my throat and stung my eyes. I'd burned the chocolate and probably broken the microwave.

"You're in big trouble. How did you manage that? Should you even be cooking when Mum and Dad aren't here?"

"Gran's here."

I knew it was stupid as I said it.

"Yeah, and how does that help exactly?"

"We were making it together but then she went out and I saw her and I went after her and I must have pressed the wrong button or something. I thought I'd stopped it. It wasn't my fault!"

"Yeah, like that's going to wash with Mum and Dad. You'd better clean it up quick and open the windows."

Gran was hovering in the doorway, wringing her hands together, and muttering something I couldn't hear.

"You're so lame. Should just stick to your toy baking set.

"I don't have a toy one. Don't be so mean."

"Really? Oh I get it. It's in the box of stuff of yours that Dad gave away to charity, isn't it?"

"What do you mean?"

"Oh, didn't you know? Well, all your stuff that didn't fit in my room has gone to charity. I've got homework to do so don't come up."

She smirked at me as she went upstairs. I felt sick. I couldn't believe Dad would have given my things away. Just because I'd put them in a box, didn't mean I didn't want them any more. It was just that it wouldn't all fit in Lou's room.

"You're LYING!"

I screamed up the stairs at her, but she slammed her door. Gran started to sing quietly,

"Down by the river,
down by the sea,
Johnny broke a bottle
and blamed it on me.
I told ma, ma told pa,
Johnny got a spanking so
ha, ha, ha."

I stared at her, and she looked at me, really clearly, like she was different somehow and she opened her arms. I went and put my head on her chest and she held me tight and squeezed me, stroking my hair. I'd missed my gran.

"Shhhh, it's OK."

I closed my eyes but the smell of burning was too strong. I had to do something before Mum and Dad came home. I pushed myself back from her and for a moment she held my gaze, her eyes watery like old people's are, then she looked around the kitchen.

"Goodness, what a mess. We'd better clear this up, young madam."

"Yep, I'll sort out the microwave. Can you put the things away? I don't really feel like making a cake now."

"Of course I can."

She didn't know where everything went, so I had to do it all. It took me ages to find the milk. She'd put it away in the cups cupboard, which was just odd. Everyone knows the milk goes in the fridge.

She went up to her room when she'd finished but I had nowhere to go so I sat at the kitchen table and started doodling. I wasn't really thinking straight but when I stopped, I realised I'd drawn smoke, loads of it, curling round and round, and hidden in the middle of the picture was me, and I was reaching my hand out for Gran, but she couldn't see me.

6

Carys and Anna think they're so cool

Katie

"Not got your slippers on today, then?"

"Or your apron?"

Carys and Anna were speaking really loudly, making sure that everyone else could hear them. I pulled a face at them and waited for Molly to put her coat away. I had to walk past Carys and Anna to get out of the cloakroom and I didn't want to do that by myself. They were blocking the exit.

"Did you bring your gran with you today? Funny how she didn't look ill, don't you think, Anna?"

"Yeah, not exactly *dying*."

"No, I thought she looked very healthy. Didn't you?"

"Yeah, I did. I guess she's just here on

holiday, then."

They were right in front of me now and there was a growing crowd around us. I could feel my skin prickling. I wished I hadn't told them anything about Gran last week. I had kind of exaggerated how ill she was, just because it didn't sound like much when I said she'd moved in with us. I tried to push past them, but Carys blocked my way and sneered at me.

"Is that right, Katie? Is your poor dying gran just here on holiday? Made up all that stuff about her being really ill, didn't you?"

And then she looked over my shoulder at Molly.

"Don't believe everything she says, Molly. She just wants attention. Isn't that right, Katie?"

She was taller than me – she was the tallest in the class – and she stepped even closer to me, so close that I could see right up her nose. Eugh. Bogie city. It made me smile. Bad move.

"Think that's funny, do you?"

She grabbed my shirt in her fist and twisted it round, her face so close to mine I could feel her breath.

"Leave it, Carys."

Molly was right behind me.

"Come on, leave her alone."

Carys let go. I pushed her out of my way and ran out of the cloakroom. I wasn't going to let her see me cry. Molly caught up with me.

"Hey, ignore her, she's just stupid."

She put her arm around me and I wiped my face with my sleeve.

"Gran *is* ill, you know."

Only she wasn't really ill, just old and a bit weird but saying she was ill was better than saying she was weird. They were right: she wasn't dying. I was never going to get my room back.

"I know. I believe you, but why were they going on about slippers?"

"Oh, it's just because Gran went out with her slippers on, so I followed her to get her to come back in, only I had my slippers on too. Then Carys and Anna turned up and started being mean and laughing."

"You mean she was actually going out for a walk in her slippers?"

"Yeah."

I looked at her and we both cracked up. It was actually kind of funny, going out for a walk in your slippers. Weird though.

It became a bit of a morning joke. Molly would say,

"So what's she done this time?"

And I'd tell her stuff, like the time she put her bra on top of her jumper and Mum had to make her get changed. Sometimes there wasn't anything to say so I made up stuff she might have done. I felt kind of bad doing that, but I bet Gran wouldn't mind. We got on. I didn't try and tell her what to do like everyone else. It was odd though, because she didn't really seem like the gran she used to be and when she did look at me, like she used to, like she really got me, it was like it made her sad. Then she'd blink and it was gone. I asked Mum about it but she just said it was old age. I added that to my List of Things Not To Do: don't get old.

7

Vera gets scared

Vera

Vera pushed the armchair against the door and then flopped into it. Still not safe. She heaved herself up and went to the windows to shut the curtains. There. No one could see in now. She turned back round to face the room and hesitated. It was dark now and she could barely see. There were shadows. She swallowed and put one trembling hand against the sofa, using it to guide her back towards the chair. The door handle turned, stopped, turned again. Her hand flew to her mouth. Someone was there.

"Vera? Vera, are you in there?"

They knew her name, knew she was in here. She didn't move. The door handle went down again and someone tried to push the door open but she was too clever for them. The armchair was heavy against the door and wouldn't budge.

"Vera? Answer me. Are you OK?"

She knew that voice. She didn't trust it. A man's voice. She shook her head, she wasn't here. Whoever it was tried again to force the door open. It opened a crack.

She moved back towards the window. Couldn't think straight. Words came to her, an old skipping song she thought. No other words.

"Oh no, here comes Miss Blackwell
with her big black stick.
Now it's time for arithmetic."

Silly, silly song but it felt right. She hummed along, louder and louder as the door gradually pushed away the armchair. The man came in. Instinctively, she backed away.

"What on earth are you doing, Vera? Let's put some lights on, shall we? I need to go and pick up Katie and Lou. Are you going to be OK, or do you want to come with me?"

Vera shook her head and watched him hesitate.

"Well, I don't like leaving you like this. Why did you put the armchair against the door?"

"Miss Blackwell with her big black stick."

"Pardon?"

"Wasn't me."

"Well, it must…oh never mind. Come on,

come with me. Come and get some fresh air."

He held his hand out and she remembered his face, but not his name. Eyes too wide apart. Lisa's husband, the girls' father. She relaxed a bit, but she didn't want to go out.

"No. I'm not coming."

"Come on, I'm sure you could do with getting out today."

"Not today, thank you. We're all fine here."

"Um…well if you're sure?"

"Quite sure, thank you. Off you go now. I've a few things to do."

She waited until she heard him leave, then she ventured out into the hallway. She went to the front door and slowly turned the doorknob, but nothing happened. She tried again. The door wouldn't open. She had to get out while there was no one here to stop her. She twisted and twisted the doorknob but it wouldn't work. Blasted door. There was a knack to it that she couldn't remember. She was frowning at it, trying to work it out when the phone rang. It took a few rings before she spotted it sitting on the dresser. She picked it up, fumbled with it, and stabbed a few buttons. There was a voice at the other end. She spoke to it in a rush.

"I can't get out. You have to come and get me. Can you hear me? I can't get out."

She stopped talking and listened. The voice

was gone. She sat down at the dining table, clutching the phone, crying.

8

Gran makes stocking stew

Katie

I was on a steam train and it was going faster and faster, so fast I couldn't see because everything through the window was blurry, but then there was a really loud shrieking noise and the train driver slammed his brakes on. I was hurtling though the carriage and the door was open and if I couldn't stop myself I was going to…

"GET UP! GET UP WILL YOU!"

My eyes snapped open. Lou was shaking my shoulders and yelling.

"What? Why? I don't…"

Lou started running down the stairs, shouting again.

"It's the smoke alarm, stupid. We need to get out."

I jumped out of bed and started to run downstairs after her. The smoke alarm was really, really loud, like it was right inside my head trying to get out. I got to the bottom of the stairs just as the bleeping stopped and just in time to see Dad shouting at Gran.

"You stupid woman! What on earth did you think you were doing?"

"Gary, don't yell at her like that!" Mum shouted.

"She nearly burned the house down! What do you expect me to do? Say 'there there don't worry?' Lisa, come on, she could have killed us all."

My heart was thumping. I'd never seen Dad shout at Gran before. He'd scared her, he was really mad with her and it made me feel funny inside. The sort of funny that they said at school you should tell a teacher about. But Dad was a teacher and he wouldn't have shouted like that unless Gran had done something really bad. Setting the house on fire was pretty bad. But I couldn't see any flames, even though the kitchen was filled with smoke. I wanted to give Gran a hug but I didn't dare.

"She's mental, you know that don't you? What's she done now?"

"Lou! How dare you talk about your gran like that."

Mum looked like she might burst, though I wasn't sure who she was more cross with: Dad, Lou or Gran. At least it wasn't me.

"Well, fair point, I'd say."

I stared at Dad. I couldn't believe he'd just said that. Lou was smirking at Mum, but Mum glared at Dad, and if she'd had knives in her eyes I'm sure they would have gone right through him.

My knees went all wobbly, so I sat on the floor. It was then that I noticed that the front door was wide open. I started to shiver as I felt the icy outdoor air curling around me. I couldn't help thinking it was a good job it was too late for anyone I knew to be walking past, because this is what I saw: Dad in his pyjama trousers furiously flapping a tea towel around the smoke alarm; Mum in her nightie, hair sticking up in tufts with her arm around Gran; Lou in her fluffy white dressing gown with her hands on her hips and Gran muttering to herself and wrapping what looked like a pile of stockings around her hands and wrists. It was almost funny. Actually it was funny, but I bit my lip so no one saw me smiling.

I wished Dad would shut the door. It was so cold and what if someone did walk past and look in? I looked at the clock on the wall. 3:10am. No one I knew would be awake at this hour, but I still wished he would shut the door. Then I noticed that the sink was full to the top with bubbles, which was a bit odd. And there was a really terrible smell like boiled up sprouts mixed with smelly socks.

"Come on, Mum. Why don't you sit down and tell us what you were doing?"

Mum pulled out a chair for Gran. Gran looked confused.

"I was just washing my stockings."

She was really starting to twist them tightly now – I could see them cutting into her skin.

"Yes, but Mum, it's 3 o'clock in the morning."

Dad was shutting the front door, shaking his head.

"Never mind the washing. Why don't you ask her what they were doing in the oven?"

Dad looked like the sticky out vein in his forehead might pop. I stared at Gran. She'd put her stockings in the oven? She'd actually cooked her stockings? No wonder the house smelt like rotten sprouts. Mum was trying to unwind the stockings from Gran's wrists. She looked like she was trying hard not to cry as she did it.

"It wasn't me."

Gran was shaking her head. She looked surprised. Lou laughed and right then, I really wanted to hit her.

"Not you? Well, who was it then?"

Mum shot Lou a stern look but she didn't say anything and as much as I hated Lou for laughing at Gran, I wanted Gran to answer her. We were all waiting for the answer.

"It was Mr. Nobody."

And that was our first introduction to him.

No one said a word. I looked at Mum, Mum looked at Dad and Dad put his hands on his head and stared right back at Mum, his eyes really big in his head.

"Oh, come *on*. I don't think even Katie has used that as an excuse."

That was from Lou and she was right: I would never have dared use that as an excuse unless I was four or something, and I still couldn't believe Gran had come out with it. But it was a pretty cool excuse for a gran.

"Now come on Mum, surely you don't expect us to believe that?"

Mum was talking to her own mum like she was a little girl. It made me feel embarrassed for Gran. Dad's vein really was going to burst if it carried on bulging like that. He looked like he wanted to break something the way he was making fists and unmaking them. Gran looked pleased with herself, like she'd just thought of the best excuse ever. It made me smile. I mean, 'Mr. Nobody'? That was just brilliant and weird at the same time. I'd have to tell Molly that on Monday.

I could just picture her face when I told her and that made me snort. It would have been a proper laugh but I was trying to hide it so it came out funny.

I only realised everyone had noticed when Dad said,

"Do you really think this is funny, Katie? Your gran put her stockings in the oven presumably because she wanted to dry them, unless she was planning a stocking stew."

I put my hand over my mouth to try and stop the giggles from bursting out of me. I couldn't help it – I had a Quentin Blake picture in my head of us eating stocking stew. I loved Quentin Blake. I wanted to illustrate children's books when I was a grown-up and I could just see how me and Quentin would draw stocking stew. Dad hadn't finished though.

"Do you have any idea how serious this is?"

I shook my head, desperately trying not to laugh. It was his fault. If he hadn't mentioned stocking stew, I wouldn't have laughed again.

"If the smoke alarm hadn't gone off and Mum hadn't raced downstairs and discovered what was going on, Gran's stockings would have probably started a fire and we may well not have been standing here discussing it now."

Dad's voice had got louder and when his fist banged on the table I managed to stop giggling. I sneaked a look at Gran who was shaking her head and looking down at the table. I wasn't laughing at her, I was laughing at the stocking stew. Mum had her head in her hands, elbows on the table. Only Lou was looking at me and she was smiling. I didn't like that she was smiling. I didn't want her to think I was like her, laughing at Gran. I turned my back on everyone and raced upstairs, two at a time, past my old room, up to Lou's.

I slammed the door and hid under the covers, feeling humiliated. We'd written a story about humiliation, so I knew what it meant to feel that way. Your cheeks burn and you get a twisted, knotted-up feeling inside and you want to disappear. It didn't last long, though. I fell asleep before Lou came back to bed and dreamt of me and Quentin tucking into a delicious stocking stew.

9

Hugo to the rescue

Katie

I'd asked Dad if I could go to the allotments with him on Saturday. I had plans for my den and I was hoping he might help. Last time we were there, I'd found some old posts and planks of wood, which he said people had used for their vegetable beds but didn't want any more, so we carried them up to our plot.

Our plot was at the end of the allotments and it backed onto the woods at the end of our road. There was a hedge between the wood and our plot but it was a thick bushy hedge, the type where you could hide in the middle if you were small enough – and I was one of the smallest in my class. I had cleared out quite a big space in the middle and I wanted to make some walls with the planks and a roof to make it cosy. I was thinking I could get some green tarpaulin to put over the top to camouflage it and keep the rain out. I knew Dad had some in his shed. He was in there getting his tools out. I think he was going to dig up some potatoes and other stuff for supper.

"Dad, can I have some of that tarpaulin, please?"

"Er, yes I guess so. What for?"

"My den. I want to make a roof."

"OK then."

"Will you help me?"

"Well, not just yet. You go and get started."

"But I…"

"No buts. Come on Katie, I've got things to do. I'll help you later. You go and work out first how you want to construct your den."

I had wanted us to do it together, but ever since the stockings incident, Dad hadn't been like Dad. It had been a week since Gran cooked her stockings and blamed Mr. Nobody and Dad hadn't talked about it since. In fact he hadn't talked a lot about anything since. Mealtimes were really quiet and if he did talk, it was either like he wasn't really listening to us or he was being polite, like he is to our friends. Mum talked to us, but not really to Dad and even Lou had stopped giving everyone so many Looks. Gran hadn't mentioned Mr. Nobody again, but sometimes when I listened outside her door, I could hear her talking to somebody. It all felt odd, in a bad way.

The hedge wasn't big enough. I didn't have

enough space to turn around and get the planks in place and I was getting scratched. It had been a stupid idea.

"Dad, I'm going into the woods for a bit."

He wasn't listening and I couldn't be bothered to go over and tell him.

"DAD! BACK LATER. I'M GOING INTO THE WOODS FOR A WALK!"

I didn't care if he heard. He should have been listening. I pushed my way out of the hedge and stood up. I hadn't been in the woods by myself before, only with Mum and Dad. We usually came in from the entrance at the top of the hill, which I was guessing was over to the left of where I was standing. I headed in that direction so I could find the path, which I hoped I would recognise. The bit I was in didn't have a path, just trees on a slope. I needed to use my hands to get up the slope because it had been raining, so it was slippy. I raced up it as fast as I could, like I was an explorer that was running out of time and had to get to the top to get some air. It would have been cool if Molly had been with me. She was great at making up games.

It was so muddy, I couldn't get a grip and I slipped part way down, making a bit of a mud slide. I thought I could get one of the planks I had in my den and use it as a mud sledge. I ran back down the rest of the slope, but when I got to the bottom it didn't look the same. I couldn't find my bit of hedge. I walked along a bit more and realised I must have gone further than I thought. I kept the hedge on my right and kept walking, but the trees were getting thicker here and it didn't feel right. I started to panic.

"DAD! DAD!"

I think the wind must have snatched my words away, so he couldn't hear me. I started to run and then I heard a dog barking. When I looked over my shoulder, I saw a Collie running towards me. I hated Collies, because they nip you like they think you're a sheep. I turned round but didn't see the root sticking out and I tripped and fell face first into the mud. I was *covered* in mud. Mum was going to go mad. But not if I couldn't find my way back to the allotments. I tried to stand up, but my ankle really hurt. At least the Collie had run off.

My ankle was throbbing now and it made me cry and the more it throbbed, the more I cried and I was lost and wet and Dad didn't even know I was here, because he couldn't be bothered to help me build my den which was a stupid idea anyway because it wouldn't fit in the hedge. I felt like my tummy had been carved out and left me with this big aching empty hollow inside which was pushing its way up into my throat. I felt sick.

A black Labrador was sniffing his way

towards me. I tried to dry my face but my sleeve was all muddy too, so I think I just smeared the tears and mud into one big mess. My ankle was still throbbing like mad, but I held out my hand to the Lab and he came closer. He seemed nervous, his tail was close to his bum, almost between his legs.

"HUGO!"

Hugo! I thought he looked familiar. It was the dog I'd met with the old lady near our house. I kept my hand out and he came closer and sniffed me. I reached over and stroked his ears and he put his head up so I stroked his chest. He loved that. He sat down next to me.

"Hugo! There you are."

Hugo got up and went to his owner, wagging his tail, before coming back to me and sniffing at my hands again. I stroked him.

"My goodness! Whatever has happened to you?"

She was wearing the same purple trousers and a purple spotty raincoat. I guessed purple was her favourite colour. I smiled, sort of.

"I tripped over and hurt my ankle."

I was trying not to cry. I could feel the tears bubbling up again in the back of my throat. I tried to stand up, but it really hurt and I yelled in pain and sat back down again. I really was crying now.

"Oh dear me, you poor love. Are your mum or dad here?"

I shook my head.

"Is anyone with you?"

I shook my head again.

"Well we'd best get you to your feet again and see if we can find you some help. Can you put any weight on it?"

I tried again and this time she helped me. I didn't want to put my foot down, though. She held onto me and Hugo stayed close, like he wanted to be near, but not too near.

"Do you know, I think Hugo likes you. He's normally so nervous around new people. I think he wants to help."

"Maybe it's because he's met me before."

She looked at me hard, searching my face and then I saw that she remembered because her eyes lit up.

"Oh yes, you were with your grandma weren't you?"

"Yep."

"That's right, I remember now. He said hello to you then, which was very unusual. There must be something about you that he likes. You're honoured."

She bent down to ruffle his fur with one hand, still holding my arm with the other. I nearly fell over and had to hop to stay next to her.

"I didn't recognise you with all that mud over you. Do you think you can manage to walk a bit? I presume you live near where we met before?"

I nodded.

"Good. Well if you can put some weight on it, then I can help you home. It's about fifteen minutes from here, though, so you'll have to be brave."

We made it home, but only because a completely random stranger helped too. It was SO embarrassing and when Mum opened the front door and saw me, I thought she was going to go mental, but she threw her arms around me, even though I was covered in mud.

It turned out that Dad hadn't been able to find me in the den and got worried and called Mum and he'd been out looking for me. She did tell me off, but I could tell she was more pleased that I was home. Mum ran me a bath and afterwards bandaged my ankle, which she said I'd sprained, and then she and I snuggled up on the sofa (with my leg on the foot stool) and watched *Harry Potter and the Philosopher's Stone*. Lou was made to take Gran out for a walk so she gave me her Cat Look. I call it that because it's like when cats are about to fight and they hiss.

When Dad got back from the allotments, he started to make supper and soon the house smelt of roast chicken. Yum. Lou and Gran came back and Gran stayed in the kitchen with Dad. Lou went up to her room of course and shut herself in. Even though I shared with her, I didn't really see what she did all day apart from play on her phone and text soppy messages to Max.

The movie finished and Mum switched off the TV. I rested my head on her arm and she moved it and put her arm around me, but didn't say anything.

"Mum?"

"Yes, love?"

"It was horrible today. I got really scared."

"I know you did."

"How do you know?"

"I could tell, and Margaret said how upset you were."

"Who's Margaret?"

"The lady who brought you home. Who do you think I meant?"

She'd never told me her name. Odd that Mum knew her name but I was the one who knew her.

"She seemed lovely. She says that her dog took a great liking to you. She also said that when you're feeling better, maybe you'd like to pop round and play with Hugo. She only lives just down the road, at number 34."

"Really? Did you say I could?"

"Yes, I did."

I squeezed into Mum's cuddle.

"Thanks Mum, you're the best."

"So are you, when you don't go running off and getting yourself covered in mud."

I looked up at Mum but she was smiling, so it was OK.

"Katie, why did you wander off by yourself?"

I shrugged.

"I dunno. Just felt like it."

"I thought you and Dad were making a den?"

"Well we were, but he didn't want to. I told him I was going for a walk instead, but he wasn't listening."

I looked at Mum again and she frowned.

"Well you should have made sure he knew where you were."

I moved out of Mum's cuddle.

"He wasn't interested. Said he had *things* to do. He's not been interested all week."

I mumbled that last bit but she heard me.

"What do you mean by that?"

"Well ever since last weekend, when Gran set off the smoke alarm, he's been acting all weird and so have you. You don't talk to each other any more."

There. I'd said it.

"I don't know what you mean. We are talking to each other."

"Not properly you're not. Just like, 'what's for tea' kind of talking. You talk to us more than to each other and you don't even do that very much at the moment."

"Katie, that's not true."

"It is. It's all because of Gran, isn't it?"

Mum sighed and shut her eyes. I thought she was going to get cross with me.

"Katie, come here. Come on."

I moved back closer and she put her arm around me again. She was going to give me a Talk.

"Listen, I'm sorry if you feel we aren't talking much at the moment. It's just there's a lot to think about and work out."

"Like what?"

"Well, like what's best for Gran, how we can look after her properly. I guess she needs more help than we thought she did and that makes it quite stressful for me and Dad."

I didn't see what made it so stressful. I mean, I was the one who'd had to move out of my room and who'd had to chase after her in the street with my slippers on and embarrass myself in front of Carys and Anna.

"I think it will be easier when we've got more of a routine going with Gran. Then we can relax a bit and then there will be more time for den building and that kind of thing. Does that sound OK?"

Not really.

"But why do you and Dad have to argue so much?"

"Katie, don't be daft. We're not arguing. Just a minute ago you said we weren't talking to each other any more."

"You know what I mean. If you're not arguing, then you're talking in cross voices. It's the same thing."

Carys' parents argue all the time. And Carys said they were going to get a divorce. I didn't want to have to choose who I lived with.

Mum held me tighter.

"Listen. You don't have to worry about me and Dad. We're fine. I'm sorry you had such a scare today, but you know, you scared us too. So maybe we all need to talk to each other a little bit more. How does that sound?"

"OK, I guess."

"Good. Well let's go and see if Dad's got that supper ready. I'm starving."

Later that night, I couldn't sleep so I bumped down the stairs on my bum (my ankle still hurt) to the bathroom to get a drink. When I got to the landing I could hear Mum and Dad's voices, so I stayed sitting on the top step and listened. They'd left the dining room door open. They were arguing again. My tummy went hard like it was trying to help me be extra still so I could hear. I heard Dad.

"We can't do it forever. It's not fair on anyone: on you, me, the girls, your mum. You know it's not. I'm sure Katie ran off today because of how she's feeling about Vera."

Not true. I'd run off today because of how I was feeling about *him*. It wasn't fair to always blame it on Gran. Though it was better when she wasn't living here.

"I'm not saying she'll stay here forever. I don't know what's going to happen, but for now she has to stay here. Or would you rather I got her admitted into one of those geriatric psychiatric wards?"

I didn't like the sound of that. Whatever it was couldn't be good from the way Mum sort of spat the words out.

"You know I'm not saying that. I'm just saying that we need to plan ahead that's all. She's already got worse so quickly and I just don't think we can cope with it. It's not just that she gets confused. She can be dangerous. I didn't know it was going to be this difficult when I agreed to take her in."

"Oh you agreed, did you? That was very

gracious of you. I didn't realise I had asked your permission."

I didn't like the way Mum's voice sounded. It made my throat feel all knotted-up. I drew my knees up to my chest and hugged them. I wanted to listen, but I didn't like the way it made me feel. Like I was back in the school cloakroom with Carys.

"Oh, don't be ridiculous. You know that's not what I mean, but do you know what? I don't think we did consider what impact this would really have on us all. And I don't think we really knew how bad her condition had got."

"She was always going to get worse. You knew that. I'm sure once she's settled in with us, she'll start to relax and things will get easier. And anyway you might not have thought about what it would really mean for us all, but I did."

I wasn't sure about that. I don't think Mum had really thought about what it was like to share with Lou while your gran slowly died in your bedroom. If she really was dying. It was more like she was loopy. Like Loopy Luna in *Harry Potter*. Dad didn't seem sure either.

"Really? So you would have anticipated the stocking incident then, when she nearly burned the house down?"

"She didn't nearly burn the house down. It was fine in the end."

I think Mum must have forgotten what that night was like. She hadn't acted like it was fine at the time. I wished they would stop. My shins hurt where my fingernails were digging in. Mum said something but I couldn't hear it.

"And what about the time she locked you out?"

I didn't know she'd done that. I wondered if she'd blamed Mr. Nobody for that too.

"Well what do you want me to do about it? I can't wave a magic wand, can I?"

I could hear Mum crying. Why didn't Dad stop? I felt tears running down my cheeks too. I don't know when they started. I wiped them away but they kept on coming. I wanted Mum and Dad to stop.

The front door slammed. I don't know who left but I couldn't go downstairs to find out, because they would see that I had been crying. Then they would know that I had been listening when I shouldn't have been. I crawled back up the stairs to bed. Lou was wide awake in bed and she smiled at me. A sorry kind of smile. Maybe she'd heard it all too.

That night I dreamed of Mr. Nobody. He was a tall man, wearing a black cloak. He had no hair, but he had a bushy black beard and cherry red eyes which were open wide and came closer and closer until I woke up suddenly, covered in sweat. My heart was thumping in my chest and I lay there for a while under the covers, before it felt safe to move. It was a relief to wake up. In my dream, he was strong and somehow bigger than his body, though I know that sounds weird. It was like he was more than just a person and I was thin and fragile, like a bird being chased by a big black cat. I drew a picture of my dream before breakfast and added it to the store of pictures under my mattress.

10

Margaret rescues Vera

Vera

Vera stepped carefully onto the pavement and hesitated, unsure whether to go down the hill or up. She chose down because it would be an easier walk.

She was tired of being cooped up like a prisoner in that house all day, guarded day and night. He'd told her that now was her chance, after Lou had gone out. She wasn't quite sure who 'he' was, so she called him Mr. Nobody. She thought it rather a fine name for him. He was a mysterious character and always seemed to be getting her into trouble. It was a wonder she listened to him, but he was the only one who really knew her, sometimes better than she knew herself. Reminded her of an Elvis song, which she started to sing:

"I'm all shook up,
I can't seem to stand on my own two feet.
Well please don't ask what's on my mind,
    I'm a little bit stuck but I feel fine."

Well, no actually, she didn't feel fine at all. She felt, well, how did the rest of it go?

My tongue gets tied when I try to speak.
My insides shake like a leaf on a tree.

Exactly! That's exactly how she felt.

"Thank you," she said to whoever had just sung those last lines for her. She supposed it was Mr. Nobody. She felt better for that and she started to hum the song as she went down the hill. She'd been so wrapped up in humming the song, bringing back lovely memories of dancing to Elvis with her girlfriends on a Friday and Saturday night (she really must arrange another night out), that she'd forgotten where she was supposed to be going. She'd reached the traffic things with the colours. Oh bother, what was it called? The cars were supposed to stop for her of course, but it was so busy and no one was stopping and the people on the other side of the road were staring at her.

She started to back away, but promptly

backed into someone who cursed. She put her head down and started walking back up the hill as fast as she could away from them all, but she was tired. She paused for breath next to a low wall at the front of someone's garden.

Just sit down here.

"Yes, I think I will."

"Excuse me?"

"Pardon?"

"I thought you said something."

There was someone in the garden she hadn't spotted when she sat down. Blast it. She supposed they would want to talk and she really wasn't in the mood. She was having a bad day, she knew that, but she couldn't for the life of her remember why.

"Are you OK, love?"

"Oh yes, thank you. We're just resting."

The bald headed man – maybe in his 70's – was leaning on his spade and looking at her strangely.

"You said 'we're'?"

"Hmmmm? Yes, I suppose I did."

How tiresome. Perhaps she should move on. But she was so tired.

"I heard you singing earlier. Elvis Presley, wasn't it?"

"Oh yes, lovely voice. In fact, I was just thinking that we needed to organise another dancing night."

"Oh you still dance, do you? Well you're doing better than me!"

The man laughed and she looked at him more closely. He was clearly far too old to go out dancing.

"Yes, I should think I am."

It didn't feel right sitting there chatting to a strange man, so she got off the wall and started to walk back up the hill.

"Would you like me to go with you?"

"No, I most certainly would not, thank you very much."

The cheek of it. She didn't need a chaperone.

"Well, it's just, if you don't mind me saying so, you don't look very appropriately dressed for this weather and I thought maybe you would welcome some company to speed up your journey home."

"Home? Oh it's not my home. It's theirs."

"I'm sorry. I don't quite understand."

She didn't have time for this fool of a man. Not dressed appropriately? Well she was cold but that's just because it *was* cold. She adjusted her dressing gown, pulling the collar up and then she noticed her feet. Slippers. She didn't have time to wonder why she was wearing her slippers, because a woman, a nurse in fact, (she had no coat on over her uniform – daft in this cold weather) was running down the hill, shouting at her. She looked vaguely familiar.

"Mum! Mum, what are you doing out here? You'll freeze. Oh, Mum! Come on, let's get you home."

'Mum', did she say?

"Now then, young lady, just you take your hands off me. I am perfectly fine, thank you. No need for a fuss. No one called for you."

"Mum, it's me, Lisa. Let's go home."

"Oh no you don't. That's not *my* home."

They had discussed this when Mr. Nobody was encouraging her to leave. She really must not let them keep her prisoner any more. She wondered if she was ill, if the home was run by nurses. Well, if she was ill, it wasn't of her own making.

"Mum, it is your home, just for now. Remember? You're living with me, Gary and the girls. Katie and Lou. Remember? Come on, you can't stay out here in your slippers and dressing gown."

Vera frowned as she looked down at herself. She couldn't remember putting those on. She started to tremble as she felt herself adrift, a fly spinning into a spider's web. The words came out of her effortlessly,

"There was an old lady who
swallowed a fly.
I don't know why she
swallowed a fly."

Someone else joined in.

"She swallowed a spider to
catch the fly."

The 'someone else' smiled at her. She had a kind face under a pink and purple knitted bobble hat.

"What a lovely hat!"

"Oh, thank you. I admit I'm a fairly keen knitter. My name's Margaret by the way."

"Very pleased to meet you, Margaret."

"Shall we walk up the road together?"

She offered her arm to Vera who took it, hesitantly. It seemed an over-familiar gesture, but she was tired. All this fuss was wearing her out.

It wasn't long before they came to a house with a blue front door and a very neat little patch of garden in the front, pansies in the borders. Such neat colourful little flowers, crimson and golden yellow. She bent down to smell them.

"Oh, what a lovely garden. You must be a keen gardener."

Margaret smiled and shook her head.

"Oh no, not me. That must be Lisa, your daughter. Look, here she is. You can ask her yourself."

Vera turned to see the person, who she presumed must be Lisa, beside them. The girl in the nurse's uniform. She felt the darkness coming in again, replacing the strings of words in her head, and leaving her with a nothingness that she couldn't explain, but it made her feel drained. Drained to the last dregs.

"Spinning, spinning, like a plate."

That's how she felt. She supposed it was him, Mr. Nobody, doing the spinning. Sometimes she suspected him of not being as nice as he could be.

She allowed herself to be led inside and an overwhelming sense of fear threatened to squeeze the breath out of her as the door shut behind her. She started to cry.

"Mum, come on, it's OK. Let's get you sat down, with a nice warm cup of tea. I'll fetch a blanket and we can tuck you up on the sofa in front of the fire."

Vera felt drowsy in front of the fire. When the nurse came back in with her cup of tea, she beckoned her to come close, so she could whisper in her ear.

"She's trying to kill me, you know."

The nurse looked startled.

"Who is?"

"She is, of course."

"Mum, what are you talking about?"

Vera widened her eyes in fear.

"He said so."

"Who said so?

"Mr. Nobody."

Carys is really mean

Katie

"Do you wanna come into town with us tomorrow morning?"

I didn't answer straight away, wondering whether they were being nice to me, or whether any minute they were going to laugh at me and run off. I tried hard to avoid them at school, but sometimes it wasn't possible, like now. Carys and Anna were standing in front of me, their arms linked like they couldn't bear to be separated. In a funny kind of way I felt sorry for Anna, because Carys was using her. She could have hung around with me and Molly but we weren't cool enough any more, apparently. Molly said Carys was a cow-faced pig and neither of them deserved to be my friend.

I should have found an answer quicker.

"Got better things to do, have you? Like

hanging around with your loopy grandma, singing nursery rhymes in the street in your nightie, maybe?"

Carys had looked at Anna when she said that and rolled her eyes. My cheeks were flaming. I could probably have burnt my finger on them they were so hot. Even worse, I was now embarrassed that I was blushing, so of course I blushed even more, right to the tips of my ears.

"How does that song go, Anna?"

"Oh, I think I know. Isn't it something to do with an old lady who swallowed a fly?"

"Why did she swallow that fly?"

"I don't know. But I do know she swallowed a spider to catch the fly."

"Oh, that's right, Anna. Hmmm. What's that next line?"

I tried to walk past them, but stupidly I'd been sitting on the tree stump in the corner of the playground next to the fence, and they'd cornered me. Carys pushed me back against the fence and laughed.

"I remember now, Anna. It's 'Perhaps she'll die'. Isn't that right, Katie? Didn't you say she was going to die?"

"Just shut up, will you?"

"Ooooh. Hit a nerve, have we? She's mad your gran. You'll probably go mad too. In fact, actually didn't we meet you in your slippers as well? You already are mad, aren't you?"

Carys came up really close, grabbed my jumper and twisted it, like she had before. I moved my head back quickly – and hit the back of my head against the fence. My eyes smarted at the unexpected pain. She sneered at me right in my face. I tried to push her off, but she was stronger than me. She smiled with her tongue between her teeth, like a snake flicking its tongue at its prey. I stared back at her, not feeling anywhere near as brave as I hoped I looked. I could feel her hot, horrible breath on my face as she spoke.

"Are we not good enough for you any more? Is that it? Maybe it's about time we told everyone what you're really like. A proper little, loopy cry baby. Boo hoo, boo hoo, my mad gran's moved in. What a baby."

All the while she was speaking, she was pressing me against the fence and I couldn't look away, but I could sense other kids around us. I wished no one else was there. I was concentrating really hard on not crying now, but she was chanting again and Anna had joined in.

"Cry baby. Cry baby. Oh no, what will I do? My gran's moved in. You loser. So what?"

"You don't know anything. Just shut up."

My voice sounded muffled to me, but even so, I knew it was shaking. I clenched my fists to try and stop the shaking that had now spread from my voice to my body. I could feel the tell-tale lump of tears in my throat.

"Just shut up."

Carys mimicked me.

This time I pushed her off and started to walk away, but she kicked the back of my legs and I stumbled. She pushed me again, harder, and I fell on the ground. I got to my knees quickly, but before I could get up completely, she pushed me again and I lost my balance and fell. She stamped her foot into my side and then she spat. A big globule of warm spit, which ran slowly down my face, like treacle. I wiped it off with my sleeve.

"Get off me!"

I pushed her foot off me. I think she must have been moving it anyway because I did it easily. I wasn't looking at her. My side really hurt where her foot had been and I could still feel her spit like it was scoring a channel in my cheek. I felt sick. I hated her.

"C'mon Carys. Let's go before someone comes."

Anna and Carys ran away laughing and I lifted my head just a fraction to see them standing with a gaggle of other girls from my class, pointing at me. I looked away and got up carefully, holding my side with one hand and wiping my face with the other. My side was throbbing. I wished Molly didn't have her flute lesson at lunchtime. They would never have dared pick on me if there were two of us. I sat by myself on the tree stump until the whistle went.

On the way home from school I was thinking about what they had said about the spider and fly rhyme, and it made me wonder if there was something I didn't know. Like Gran had been out by herself again, singing, and they'd seen her. It was kind of funny in the house, but not outside, not where other people could see you. Lou hated taking Gran out for a walk in case she embarrassed her.

I was the first one home. Sometimes I wondered if Gran had come to live with us so that Mum could be late home from work. I mean, I wasn't a baby so I didn't need babysitting, but Mum said I was too young to be at home by myself so usually I went to After School Club. Now Gran was here, I was allowed to come home straight after school some nights instead. But the thing is, no one trusted Gran to look after herself so how could that mean they trusted her to look after me? Didn't make sense, especially when Mum and Dad told *me* to keep an eye on *her*.

I let myself in and it was all quiet. I shut the door carefully behind me. Dad said we had to be sure it was always shut, though Gran wasn't stupid – she knew how to open a door. Well, most of the time she did. He said he was going to get us keys and keep it locked all the time, but Mum said he couldn't lock Gran in because what if there was a fire? I didn't want to live in a prison anyway.

I dumped my bag by the door. I had homework but I'd do it later. I got some squash and opened the biscuit tin. It had been half full yesterday but now there were only a few biscuits left. We all thought Gran was eating them during the day, especially after Mum found the lunch she'd left for Gran dumped in one of the plant pots. Of course Gran blamed Mr. Nobody. I quite liked Mr. Nobody – he and Gran were more fun than anybody else in my house.

I ate all the biscuits in the tin. There were four and we were only allowed two each, but Mum would think Gran had eaten them so it didn't matter. Gran didn't seem to care when Mum accused her of something. She just smiled and either walked away or blamed Mr. Nobody. Sometimes she would smile at me, like she and I had done something bad together and I would smile back because I liked it better when she smiled. But if Lou saw me, she'd give me The Look. The 'You're Such A Baby' Look. I wish I had a baby sister, instead of a grumpy teenager one.

I went upstairs, paused outside Gran's room and heard her snoring. I carried on up to Lou's room. It didn't feel right calling it my room, because it wasn't. I sat at Lou's desk in her spinny chair and spun round and round until I was dizzy. She'd hate it if she knew, so I did it again and again until I felt a bit sick. I opened her desk drawers. Boring. She had some nice pens though, and paper, which I might borrow another time. I wasn't in the right mood for drawing right now.

I don't know what I was looking for, really. It was just that I knew I had half an hour before she got home from school, so I could do what I wanted. I reached into the back of the bottom drawer and felt a hard book with some kind of metal thing on it. I pulled it out. It looked like a diary and it was locked. I wondered where the key would be. She didn't have a treasure box like me to keep it in. I'd never seen her write in it. I made a promise to myself that I would stay up late and pretend to be asleep so I could see where she kept the key. Though I wasn't sure I would read it if I found the key. Maybe I would.

"Now there are three steps to Heaven.
Just listen and you will plainly see."

Gran had woken up and put music on at full volume. I shoved the diary back in the drawer and ran down the stairs, two at a time. Mrs. Branscombe next door had complained about the noise the other day.

"Gran! Turn it down!"

Gran was dancing. I had never seen her dance before. She looked really funny. She was wearing the brown skirt that she seemed to always wear, a stripy jumper and on top of that, a lacy black bra and she was waving a scarf around. She couldn't hear me so I turned the volume down and then she noticed me.

"Oh, hello my love. We're just getting ready to go out."

I hoped she wasn't. Not with her bra on like that. That would be SO embarrassing.

"Where are you going?"

"Oh, out. It's the girls' night out. They'll be here any minute and I really must get myself ready."

There was a really bad smell in my room.

"Have you seen my hat?"

"Uh, no, sorry. What does it look like?"

"Oh be a love and help me find it."

"OK."

Anything to stop her going outside. I opened the wardrobe door and the smell hit me. It was like the smell of the worst poo you've ever done.

Surely she hadn't? I turned away and held my breath. It was then that I noticed the dark marks on the carpet. My carpet had never had dark marks on it. It was a light brown carpet; we had the same throughout the house. Gran had stopped dancing and flopped into her armchair.

"Oh goodness me, I'm worn out. I'd better have a rest before they get here."

I had no idea what she was talking about, but sometimes it was best just to pretend I understood. She always got cross when Mum and Dad told her she was wrong. Lou tended to avoid her, because she was always telling Lou to 'take that look off your face' and laughing. Mum said it was because it was a line from a song that Gran remembered. She remembered more songs than she did anything else. If you just agreed with Gran, it was like having a part in a play. I wasn't sure what my part was yet. Yesterday I think I had played Mum because Gran kept calling me Lisa.

"Who's coming, Gran?"

"Oh you know, *they* are."

"Your friends you mean?"

"Yes, yes that's right. Oh my hat. Where's my hat?"

"In the wardrobe probably, Gran."

I turned back to the wardrobe and held my nose. It really stank. I could see the hat, which had been turned upside down. It was her pink beret, only it wasn't pink on the inside. It was kind of spotty, it looked like. Brown spots. UGH! They weren't spots. I backed away and thought I might be sick. It was in *my* wardrobe. In *my* room. AND on *my* carpet. Gran had pooed in her hat!

"Have you found it, dear?"

I shook my head and ran out of the room.

12

We have a family conference

Katie

Aunt Sal was here and she'd brought the twins. Uncle Steve was away this weekend she said, so she'd come by herself. She wasn't staying though. She'd just come for Sunday lunch.

Lou said Mum had made her come, because they had to discuss what to do about Gran. It wasn't just the poo. Gran was refusing to wash and kept going out by herself and getting lost and people would bring her home. It seemed lots of people on our road knew where she lived. People I'd never met before. Gran seemed to know them all. Sometimes Margaret brought her back. Mum said I could go out later and visit Margaret and Hugo, so I'd rung her and she said we could take Hugo for a walk if I got there by mid afternoon.

Dad had cleared away the plates and was making coffee. Gran was snoring in the armchair in the lounge. She'd had two glasses of wine. I think maybe Dad had filled her glass up on purpose so she would fall asleep. The twins had finally gone to sleep after Aunt Sal had put them in the pushchair and rocked them forever. Normally I'd go and read a book or draw or something, but I wanted to hear what they were going to say about Gran. Lou was still at the table too.

"Katie, why don't you go up to your room for a bit?"

Why should I? They didn't say that to Lou.

"I don't want to."

"Well, we're going to be talking."

I shrugged and did my best Lou Look. I was staying.

"I'll do some drawing here. I don't have my own desk any more."

I got up to get some paper and pens and saw Aunt Sal raise her eyebrows at Mum.

"Oh, I've got it all to come, haven't I? Those difficult pre-teen years."

Aunt Sal was annoying. I sat down and started doodling.

Dad sat down too and poured the coffee. No one said anything. I kept my head down. It was like in assembly when Mrs. Judd asked who'd like to put up their hands to admit they'd done something. Everybody was waiting for everyone else. It was Dad who broke the silence.

"So Sal, what do you think?"

"Well, she seems OK to me. I'll admit she seems a bit scatty and definitely forgetful, but she's been perfectly pleasant."

I looked at Lou and she rolled her eyes. Mum put a warning hand on Lou's arm.

"She can have conversations. She remembers polite phrases and uses them in the right context and that works when you don't see her very often. If you lived with her, then you'd realise she's putting on an act. For you."

Mum's voice sounded strained. It was her 'trying to be patient' voice. She was right, Gran was a good actress. Some days she didn't seem so mad and today was one of those days. She'd been great with the twins, really silly with them and although she kept asking Aunt Sal the same questions, the questions made sense.

"Well, that's what you say but I have spoken to her you know, over the phone."

I saw the look that passed between Mum and Dad and held my breath. I don't think they knew that Gran had used the phone.

"And I have to say, she seemed perfectly lucid. And, well, she was scared. Of you, I'm afraid to say."

Aunt Sal stopped and looked at Mum and Dad, but Mum was shaking her head and Dad had his hands open wide and a look that said, "You really are stupid." He didn't like Aunt Sal much. She carried on.

"Yes, she said something about you locking her in and keeping her prisoner?"

"That's complete nonsense. She has difficulty opening the door because you have to pull the handle down and turn the knob, and some days she can't manage that. You know what though, maybe we *should* lock her in to stop her wandering off and getting lost."

Dad's vein was starting to throb. Always a sign that you should stop talking. It seemed that Aunt Sal didn't realise that.

"Well, I certainly don't think there's any need for that. Have you told *her* that too? Have you not thought that maybe she's just reacting to the way you treat her?"

"We treat her very well, thank you very much. How DARE you come here and accuse us of mistreating her. You have absolutely no idea."

Mum's voice was getting louder. She didn't often get cross like this.

"You haven't got a clue, have you? You never visit, you talk to her, what once on the phone, and suddenly you're the expert?"

"Lou! Please stay out of this."

Mum had pink anger spots on her cheeks.

"No, she needs to know."

Mum shrugged as if she was saying OK to Lou. She NEVER let Lou speak like this to anyone normally. I stopped doodling.

"Listen, I think we should all calm down. I'm not accusing you of mistreating her. I'm just trying to get to the bottom of what's going on here."

Dad's turn now.

"What's 'going on here' is that your mother needs more help than we can give her. She's a danger to herself and to us. For goodness sake, she nearly burned the house down a few weeks ago, or did you forget that?"

Aunt Sal looked uncomfortable. Good.

"Yeah and she did a massive poo in Katie's wardrobe."

"Lou! Please!"

"Well, she did."

Aunt Sal looked at me. I nodded.

"It stank."

They all ignored me.

"She can't dress herself properly. She can't cook. She throws away the food I leave for her. She gets up in the night thinking it's day. She doesn't know who I am most of the time."

Mum stopped. She was crying. Lou put her

arm around her. I watched them and had a funny feeling in my tummy. I didn't know she'd been getting up in the night and I didn't realise Mum was that upset. I'd never seen Lou like that with Mum. *I* wanted to comfort her. My eyes started to prickle. Dad came and put his arms around me and turned to Aunt Sal at the same time.

"Just look, will you? Look at what this is doing to us. Does it look right to you?"

He kissed the top of my head and I started crying properly, because I wasn't crying about Gran and Dad thought I was. I was crying because I felt left out. Like I didn't belong. That same feeling I'd had since I'd moved out of my room was getting stronger and I didn't like it. I wiped my eyes and looked at my doodle. It was a man with a big coat, a bushy beard and huge red eyes. Mr. Nobody. And in a lighter outline, just kind of floating at the edge of the page was a girl with long dark hair in trousers, wellies and a hooded top. Me. I coloured her in to make her stronger, somehow.

13

The Decision

Katie

I'd been to Margaret's a few times since that day she rescued me from the woods. She always had something delicious that she'd just taken out of the oven when I got there. We'd go for a walk with Hugo and then come back and eat whatever she'd cooked. My favourite was her Victoria Sponge. I told her she was like Mary Berry but she laughed and said I was too kind. It was true though – she was a great baker and she was just really nice. Mrs. Jackson tells me off for using 'nice' in my descriptions, but it was the perfect word for Margaret.

I didn't have to pretend with her, I could just be me. Somehow, I always told Margaret what was going on without her asking me, and she always listened. She never really told me what to do, but I always felt better. Today I was telling her about The Decision.

"They're selling Gran's house so they have enough money to put her in a nursing home."

I didn't think it was fair. It was Gran's house, not theirs. And she wasn't a pet; you couldn't just give her up and give her to a Gran rescue centre. Actually, that would be pretty funny. I could see the Quentin Blake picture in my head of all the grans that nobody wanted any more, left at the entrance, demanding more tea or something. I bit my lip to stop myself from smiling. I wanted to know what Margaret thought.

"Well, that must have been a very hard decision to make. Hard for your Mum especially."

I thought about it for a moment.

"Yeah, it was Dad's idea, not Mum's. I don't think she's very happy about it, but she says we can't keep on looking after Gran forever."

"It's probably for the best, for all of you. Your mum and dad must be ever so worried about her when they're at work and it can't be nice for your gran either. And I know it's hard on you and your sister."

I thought about Gran. She was always happy to see me, but she was acting weirder all the time and had started actually talking out loud to Mr. Nobody. I'd heard her. She didn't seem to like Dad either, but then I don't think he liked her. He was always telling Mum that they had to *do* something about her. As for Lou, she was just Lou. She was just the same grumpy that she always had been. Apart from the fact that she was being nice to Mum. I was *always* nice to Mum, but Lou being nice to Mum meant that they had chats together and when I came into the room, they'd change the subject. Maybe it was better if Gran went, then things could be like how they used to be. Lou said I would always have poo stains on my carpet. I'd ask Mum and Dad for a new one, though.

"Penny for them?"

"Pardon?"

"Penny for your thoughts! You were miles away then."

"Oh, I was just thinking that maybe you're right, maybe it would be best for everyone if she went into a home."

I felt bad not telling her exactly what I was thinking, but then some things are best kept secret, even from Margaret. Sometimes I thought she could read my mind anyway.

14

Vera doesn't trust Lisa

Vera

Vera took the pills from Lisa and popped them into her mouth. With her tongue she pushed them to the side, behind her teeth. Lisa turned around to put the pills back in the cupboard and Vera quickly hooked the pills out of her mouth and pushed them into her pocket. She took a quick slurp of tea, heart beating fast at her daring.

"Steady Mum, it's probably still hot."

"Oh, don't fuss so. I think I'll take a walk this afternoon."

"That sounds like a good plan. I'll get one of the girls to go with you."

"No need. I'll be fine by myself."

"Nice to have some company, though."

"No it won't. I'll go by myself."

Honestly. This woman always thought she

knew best. She was in uniform. A nurse of sorts, she supposed. More like a prison warden. Still, she couldn't make a fool out of her. Those pills were making her drowsy and she needed her wits about her. They couldn't be trusted.

Who couldn't?

"The others. They can't be trusted, that's what I said."

"Pardon, Mum?"

"Oh never you mind."

"Mum, who were you talking to just then?"

Vera frowned. She wasn't going to tell.

"Mum, you do know it's just me and you downstairs, don't you?"

She was trying to trick her, obviously.

"I'm not a fool, you know."

"No one's saying you're a fool. We just want to help you and we can't if you won't talk to us."

Go on, tell her about me. She won't believe you anyway.

"Well, if you must know, I was talking to Mr. Nobody."

Vera folded her arms across her chest and glared at the nurse. The nurse shook her head.

"Mum, we're not fools either. You can't blame everything on Mr. Nobody."

15

Lou hates me and Gran

Katie

On Wednesdays I went to Molly's after school. Sometimes Molly came to our house, but usually only at weekends, because during the week I was at After School Club, or sometimes at home with Gran.

I didn't really want anyone coming over now anyway. I didn't have a bedroom I could go to and Gran would probably do something weird. It was OK if it was just me and her (unless it was a poo thing) but if other people were there it felt different. Embarrassing. Then I felt bad that I was embarrassed, so really it was just better if I didn't invite anyone over. Dad didn't get it. Parents can be pretty stupid sometimes. I don't mean that in a bad way, but I hope when I'm a parent I won't forget what it's like to be me.

Dad had come to pick me up from Molly's

and was chatting to her mum.

"Thanks for having her. You really must send Molly over to us again soon. She's not been over for a while, has she, Katie?"

Molly and I exchanged looks. We'd agreed it was better if we played at her house, because mine was a danger zone with Gran and what she might do next. I felt my cheeks burn as I thought about it. I felt bad for Gran, like I was betraying her.

"Well that would be lovely, wouldn't it, Molly?"

Molly kind of shrugged and rolled her eyes at her mum.

"Come on then, Katie, let's get home and see what your gran's been up to."

Molly smirked at me, but I turned away because I didn't want Dad to think I'd been saying stuff about Gran.

"See you, Molly."

"Yeah, see you."

Dad and I got into the car.

"You two fallen out or something?"

"No. Why?"

"Oh, well she didn't seem too keen to come over."

I shrugged and looked out of the window.

"Your mum's worried about you, you know. We both are. You haven't been out with your friends for ages. Has something happened that you want to tell us about?"

Well, yeah. Gran moved in, remember? Couldn't he work out what was wrong?

"I can't invite anyone over Dad, can I?"

"Why not?"

He looked really confused but it was SO obvious.

"Because I don't have a room any more, do I? And I have a gran who's just weird and might do something odd or stupid or something."

"Is that really how you feel? Is that why none of your friends have been over?"

Duh!

"Yes."

I couldn't understand how he didn't realise. Surely it was obvious that I wouldn't want anyone to come home any more. He looked away like he didn't want me to see his eyes. They were watery. I didn't want Dad to cry, though. It wasn't what Dad did.

"We thought you must have fallen out with your friends. I hadn't realised you just didn't want to bring them home. Katie, listen, I'm sure we can arrange to get Gran and Lou out of the way for a bit if you want some space with your friends. You shouldn't feel you can't invite anyone round."

"Maybe."

I didn't want to tell him about Carys and Anna. I only had Molly left who I could invite. I should go out with Molly more, but I'd got into the habit of visiting Margaret at the weekends. Her house was beginning to feel more like home than my house. But maybe if he really meant it, about getting Gran and Lou out of the way, then I'd ask Molly over again. I kind of missed playing with her.

"Sometimes you just have to talk about what's bothering you so we can help."

I shut my eyes in the car. I didn't want to talk. He was wrong. If you talked about it, it became worse. If it stayed in your head, then you could keep it in. If you let your thoughts out when they were still only baby angry thoughts, you couldn't tell where the words would end up.

When we got home, the house stank. Dad went round opening all the windows with an expression on his face like he'd swallowed something disgusting. Because it was going to be a while until they could sell Gran's house and find her a nursing home, Mum had got the 'meals-on-wheels' people to come round every day while we were all out. She didn't want Gran using the oven, she said. I didn't want her eating all the biscuits either, so it seemed like a good idea, but she still ate all the biscuits and the house now stank every day.

If I was Gran I would have complained by now. The meals all smelt like the worst school dinner rice pudding, which had been kept warm all afternoon, until it festered. I loved the word 'festered'. It made me think of bubbling green scaly creatures with snake tongues and big bulging eyes. I'd drawn a picture of one of those creatures coming out of the tin foil that Gran's meals came in. The creature's face looked a little bit like Carys.

I liked to imagine the meals-on-wheels people roller-skating up to the house, holding the meal up high above their shoulders in one hand and ringing the bell with the other. I could see them in pink mini-skirts and silver sparkly jackets. That's the uniform I would give them to cheer up all the old people they took food to. I think actually though, they were people like Carys' mum. They wore *sensible* clothes. That's what Mum said. Sensible means boring. Mum says I have a really vivid imagination. So does Mrs. Jackson though she says it like it's a good thing. Mum doesn't always say it like Mrs. Jackson does.

Lou was at Max's "doing an art project". Yeah, right. Probably kissing. Ugh. I quite liked Max, he was always nice to me. Not like Lou. I couldn't understand why he went out with her. They were always laughing at stuff. She never laughed at the jokes I told her. Mum thought he was polite and even Dad liked him, but not enough to let Lou go round on a weekday. Seemed that he didn't mind this week, though.

"Have you got some homework to do, Katie?"

"Not really. I mean, I don't need to do it tonight."

"Well, I was just going to suggest that you could get on with it while I get supper sorted since Lou's out. You'll have the room to yourself."

"OK."

I knew exactly what I was going to do, though. I'd seen where Lou kept her key for her diary. If she hadn't always been having private chats with Mum then I wouldn't have looked, but it wasn't fair. Why should I always be the one who was left out?

I ran upstairs and emptied the pen pot that was on Lou's desk. The key came tinkling out. I got the diary, unlocked it, and then sat down on my bed with it.

I had to count up to 100 before I could open it. It was wrong to open someone's diary. I knew that, of course I did, but this was different. I had to find out what she and Mum were always talking about.

I skipped through a few pages until I saw

my name and my heart jumped. Should I read it?
I did.

Dear Diary,

  *What an annoying stupid babyish little pest of a
sister I have. None of my friends have to share their
room with their baby sisters. It's so not fair. Katie just
smiles at me in that really aggravating smug way she
has. She's such a daddy's darling. Can't stand it.
Don't know why they're always making a fuss of her.
She is such a stupid baby. I hate her.*

I covered the page with my hand before
flicking on through a few more pages. I wasn't
going to think about it, that wasn't why I was
looking in the diary. She was really horrible
sometimes. Well, most of the time. She couldn't
really hate me, could she? I felt a bit sick. I wasn't
sure I wanted to read any more, but I flicked
through a few more pages. The diary was pretty
boring actually and I'd almost given up finding
anything other than how much she loved Max,
who all her stupid friends fancied, how annoying
Gran was and how much she had a crush on Mr.
Dean. That bit was interesting. I'd remember that
for later. You never knew when it might be
useful. Then I found what I was looking for.

Dear Diary,

I heard mum and gran arguing today. Gran accused mum of stealing all her money, which is rubbish. Mum tried to tell her it wasn't true, but gran wouldn't listen to her and started shouting at her. I came down the stairs, but I stayed out of sight because gran hates me. I didn't want to make it worse. Then mum said something like, 'I'm your daughter. I am just trying to help you.' And gran said, 'don't you pretend you're my daughter. I've never met you before. All I know is that you want my money and I'm not giving it to you.' I couldn't believe it and then you'll never guess what – gran actually threw a vase at mum. It missed, but what if it hadn't missed? Gran came up the stairs past me and she looked really pleased with herself. I went into the lounge and found mum crying her eyes out. It was horrible. I HATE gran. I've never seen mum like that. I cleaned up the glass for her and gave her a cuddle and she cried and cried. I HATE gran. Dad's right, she needs to go into a home. I don't understand why mum doesn't want her to go. She's horrible to mum. I HATE HER!!!!!

I felt all sweaty and sort of echoey. I didn't have time to read any more because Dad was calling me for tea. I shut the diary, locked it and put it back carefully where I'd found it. Why didn't I know any of this? I couldn't believe it. Why didn't anyone tell me? Did Dad know?

I couldn't look at Gran at supper. I ate quickly and asked to leave the table. Dad said I could. Mum was working late tonight so it had just been us three at the table and Dad and I let Gran talk. She was in one of her funny moods, like comical funny not weird funny (well maybe a little weird) and normally I would have laughed along, but not tonight. Not now that I knew what she'd done.

I went to bed early but before I did, I drew a picture of Gran throwing a vase at Mum. Behind her was Mr. Nobody and he was holding her throwing arm, like he was helping. I hated both of them.

16

Mr. Nobody is really scary

Katie

"AAAAAGH!!"

I woke up when Mr. Nobody's eyes were right in front of mine. I felt him breathing on me. I screamed again. He was definitely there. He was on top of me.

"AAAAAGH!"

"Shut up, Katie!"

"AAAAAGH!"

Lou? Was that Lou?

"Katie calm down. Stop it, will you?"

Me stop? I couldn't move. *Lou* was on top of me.

"AAAAAGH! AAAAAGH!"

"Stop it, Katie. Stop it!"

Her hand made a noise on my cheek like a

wet fish hitting a chopping board. I didn't scream again. I stared at her. She'd hit me. I felt my cheek where it was burning with Lou's handprint.

"Katie, you were having a nightmare. I'm sorry I slapped you, but you wouldn't stop screaming. It's OK. You're awake now."

I was breathing really fast and I was sweaty all over. Lou was talking to me like she was miles away or talking on a phone with a really bad signal. My ears were all blocked up. Lou moved off me and sat on the side of my bed. I sat up slowly and looked at her, but she wasn't giving me one of her Looks. She looked almost like she was worried about me. Weird.

"What were you dreaming about?"

"Him. Mr. Nobody."

"Mr. Nobody?"

That was more like Lou. She was giving me her "You Can't Be Serious" Look. Dad calls that her 'McEnroe Look' after some tennis player who apparently always shouted that when he lost a point. I didn't believe him, but if you Google "You cannot be serious", his name comes up first and you can watch a YouTube clip of him doing it. Sometimes, just to annoy her, I mimic McEnroe when she gives me her Look. She hates it when I do that. I didn't do it now though, I had to explain my nightmare before it disappeared back into my head.

"Yeah. He was chasing me and laughing, and when Gran looked at me she looked at me with his eyes, and it was like he was making her move like she was a puppet, and he was chasing me out of the house and they were both laughing, but then Gran was crying, and he made her raise her hand and she was holding something but I couldn't see what, and she was going to throw it at me and I screamed and I…I think that's when I woke up."

I hadn't noticed Mum come into the room while I'd been talking. The words had all come out in one big lump so I was out of breath and shaking. Lou was smiling and shaking her head, like she knew more than me.

"He's not real, you know. It's just Gran's excuse when she's done something she shouldn't have."

Mum sat down next to me and pulled me in close for a cuddle.

"She's right, Katie. He's not real, it's just a dream."

"But it's true, isn't it? Gran did throw something at you Mum, didn't she?"

I caught Mum glancing at Lou and Lou widening her eyes and shaking her head.

"It is true, isn't it?"

Mum sighed and stroked my head. Lou was looking at me suspiciously. I quickly buried my head in Mum's nightie. I didn't want Lou to realise I'd read her diary.

"Shhhh. It's OK, Katie. That was an accident. Sometimes Gran does things that she doesn't mean to do. It's not really Gran doing those things. You just have to remember that."

I sat back. She knew then. I said it out loud just to be sure.

"I know. It's Mr. Nobody."

Mum smiled like I was joking, but I was being serious. I'd been thinking about it. I mean why was it that Gran was getting worse and she was always blaming Mr. Nobody? *And* I'd heard her speaking to him. *And* when I was doodling, he just came out of my pencil even though I wasn't thinking about him. *And* now he'd come into my dream and turned it into a nightmare. *And* I *knew* that Gran wouldn't be that nasty to Mum.

"No, I mean it, Mum. He's not just an excuse. You just said it's not Gran doing it."

"I didn't mean it like that, Katie. I meant that Gran's not well and so that makes her do things that she wouldn't normally do."

"Katie, it was just a nightmare. Anyway, she won't be here for much longer. Tell her, Mum."

Another secret between Mum and Lou? Since when did they tell each other everything and leave me out?

"Well, that's not strictly true. What Lou means is that we have a buyer for Gran's house and your dad and I are going to look at a few nursing homes. It could be months, though, before there's a place available for her. In the meantime, we just have to look after Gran as best we can and remember that she's ill and that's why she's behaving the way she does. OK? She doesn't realise what she's doing half the time."

I nodded, but my heart was knocking on my chest like it wanted to jump out and scream at Mum. Maybe this was all part of the plan? Maybe if Mr. Nobody made her so totally weird, we'd be forced to put Gran into one of those homes. I couldn't get rid of a really scary thought. What if when Gran went, Mr. Nobody stayed? What if I got my room back but he stayed in it? I shivered at the thought. I think I'd prefer Gran to Mr. Nobody.

"Come on, let's get you back under the covers and back to sleep. It'll all be OK. You too Lou, back to bed."

Lou got into her bed and I buried myself under my covers.

"Night, girls."

"Night, Mum."

I shut my eyes and everything went into cherry red pinpricks, the colour of his eyes. I didn't trust him. I buried my face in my pillow to try to block him out. The pin pricks turned into shooting stars and the more they shot across my eyelids, the more my chest felt like it was filling with something heavy and fizzing and explosive, and it was going to spill out and there was nothing I could do to stop it. I started to cry, explosive bursts of tears that I couldn't control and then I felt Lou stroking my head and shushing me. She lay down next to me and held me until I fell asleep.

17

Margaret gives me a picture

Katie

I made a promise to myself that I wouldn't read Lou's diary again unless she was totally mean to me. She still gave me a Look every now and then, but I'd counted and it was no more than four times a day, which was a massive difference.

I wasn't sure why she was being nice to me and sometimes even smiling at me, but I was being nice back just in case. It freaked me out a bit. I mean she wasn't used to smiling unless it was at Max when she did this silly teenager, "oh I Lurve You" Look. I decided I wouldn't wind her up so much. Though maybe I would check out her diary after all, to find out why she was really being nice. I'd always wanted a pretend big sister or brother, like Charlie in *Charlie and Lola*. You could tell he was a made up character because he was far too nice to his little sister.

Dad was going on a training course, so he had time to drop me off at school on his way. Mum had obviously told him about the nightmare because he told me not to worry about Gran, that it would all be OK. I wondered who was talking to Gran, telling *her* it would all be OK. It was like she was there, but not there. Maybe I should try and talk to her. She might listen to me.

Luckily I spotted Molly at the school gate when we got there, so I didn't have to walk in by myself. I didn't like going anywhere in school by myself in case I walked into Carys and Anna. Carys hadn't hurt me again, but she called me names and always made a point of being mean to me in front of everyone else whenever she saw me. She wasn't stupid though, she never did it in front of the teachers. I was trying out Lou's Looks on her but I was rubbish at it. She just laughed at me. I saw her laugh at Anna the other day and I almost felt sorry for her, but then I didn't.

It was Literacy with Mrs. Jackson and we were working on poems.

"Right then everybody. Listen up. Your homework assignment is to write a poem."

There was a massive groan, me too. I liked poems and writing but I didn't like homework. It was boring.

"You'll be pleased to know that I'm giving you two weeks to do this so you can take your time over it and weave in all those lovely words and expressions you've been experimenting with in class."

Molly looked at me and made a sad face. I shrugged back. Actually two weeks wasn't so bad and at least it wasn't one of those boring sheets of sentences she kept giving us to complete.

"The topic of your poem is 'a person close to you.' So I want you all to think of someone you are close to – it can be a relative or a friend; it doesn't matter who – and I want you to think of how you would describe that person and what is it about them that makes you laugh or smile, or annoys you or angers you. Maybe they make you feel both happy *and* sad. Tell us how they do that."

Molly and I looked at each other. I wondered if she was thinking the same as me. Carys annoyed me, but she wasn't close to me any more, so maybe she wasn't a good choice. Bet I could write a good poem about how annoying and mean she was, though.

"And just to make it interesting, we are going to have a poetry reading where you will be able to read your own poems out to the rest of the class. There will be prizes, not just for the way you write your poems, but the way you *read* them."

Mrs. Jackson grinned at us. A grin a bit like the wolf's in *Little Red Riding Hood*. Nightmare. I didn't mind (too much) writing a poem for Mrs. Jackson to read, but not for the whole class to hear. I definitely wasn't going to write about Carys now. That was going to be the worst day ever. Maybe Gran would burn the house down or something and I wouldn't have to go to school that week. Knowing Mum and Dad, they'd probably make me come anyway.

"Let's have a go at reading out some poems today to get you in the mood."

More groans.

I went to Margaret's after school. She had swapped her purple combats for red cords and a red and white stripy jumper, which kind of matched her red cheeks and white hair. I loved Margaret's house. It felt so warm and colourful and friendly, like a proper home. It wasn't neat and tidy like ours (though ours was less neat now Gran lived there). Sometimes I would daydream about living in her house as if she were my gran and I was having a sleepover. She'd be way more fun as a gran than Gran was.

We always chatted in her lounge, which she

called her 'front room'. I guess that was because it was at the front of the house, although she did also have another room at the front. Weird. Anyway this room was all reds and oranges and there was stuff everywhere. She had random patterned rugs on the floor and pictures on the wall, all of patterns and landscapes in weird shapes. She usually had the fire going which was a real fire. Dad said real fires were a pain and messy but he was wrong because this fire was just cosy. I loved watching the flames as they bounced and twirled around the wood when she put new logs on. She had candles on the mantelpiece too. We used to have candles at home, but Dad says they're too much of a fire risk now.

I wished I could live in Margaret's house where you didn't have to be careful about things; you could just live there. I'd miss Mum and Dad though. And probably Lou now. And maybe Gran a little bit, especially when she was being funny and singing along to Elvis.

I'd been telling Margaret about my dream. I even told her what I thought about Mr. Nobody's powers and she didn't laugh at me.

"Dreams are just a way of your brain working out what's been going on. Sometimes your head gets too full in the daytime and your brain needs the peace and quiet of your sleeping time to put all the little connections together between thoughts and events and help you work out what to think."

"So does it mean that Mr. Nobody really does exist then?"

Margaret thought about this for a minute.

"Well, I'd say that Mr. Nobody is obviously real for your gran."

I nodded and bent down to rub Hugo's tummy. He was lying on my feet with his feet up in the air making a funny kind of dog purring noise.

"I've drawn pictures of Mr. Nobody you know, but no one in my family believes he exists."

"Well the great thing about drawings is that they work a bit like dreams in some respects. They help you to extract the muddle in your mind and display it in all its glory on a page."

I didn't think there was much glory about Mr. Nobody, but I didn't interrupt. I liked listening to Margaret's voice and stroking Hugo at the same time. It was like being wrapped up in a big warm fleecy blanket.

"Come on, I'll show you."

Hugo jumped up to follow Margaret, so I did too, though I wasn't sure what she wanted to show me. She led the way to the other front room, the one I'd not been in yet. It was so different. It was totally white: the floorboards, the walls, the blinds – but not bright white. It was like a calming white, almost grey-white.

There was a huge easel in the middle of the room with a painting on it, but it wasn't finished. It was a countryside scene, only the colours weren't proper greens and browns, they were turquoises and ambers. The outlines weren't proper tree outlines either, it was more like the trees were characters in a movie and looked like they might get up and walk out of the painting. I stared into the painting for ages before I looked around the room.

"This is my painting den."

Margaret laughed and threw her arms out to show me the room. It explained why she wore colourful clothes. There was paint everywhere: splashes of it on the floor, on the two tables near the easel, on some clothes dumped on a chair in the corner, on some purple Crocs next to the chair, on the bookcase, on a stripy apron on the floor next to the easel. There were paint pots on the tables and crammed into the bookshelf. Alongside them, were brushes and plastic bottles filled with clear liquid, sketch pads, rags, books and stacks of magazines. There were even more magazines in piles on the floor by the wall. There was a sink in the corner and then I saw, against the wall, paintings stacked up, all different sizes.

I went over to them and ran my finger along the top of the picture nearest to me.

"Those are the ones waiting for frames. I've a lot more upstairs. Feel free, have a look through."

How awesome was that! A granny painter. She'd shown me pictures of her grandchildren, so I knew she was a granny. There were some kids' pictures stuck to a pin board above the sink, so I was guessing they were done by her grandchildren. They must really miss her. She said that they lived in Germany so she didn't see them very much. I felt sorry for her when she told me, because she looked so sad. I wondered if my gran would miss me when she was sent to the home. I wasn't so sure. Most of the time I don't think she even knew who I was. She definitely liked me more than Lou, though.

"There is a certain kind of magic in pictures. It's my secret therapy. When I can't get the words out, or when I can't resolve something that's nagging at me, I reach for my pens or paints and I give myself over to another world. It is a bit like being possessed by a power I can't control. My conscious mind takes a back seat and lets my unconscious mind take over, just like when we dream. So when you are drawing your Mr. Nobody, you are giving voice to the thing that is niggling away at the back of your mind."

I didn't like to think of Mr. Nobody living at

the back of my mind, but what she said did kind of make sense. I didn't mean to draw Mr. Nobody or dream about him, he just appeared without me making it happen.

"I believe that there is no such thing as an idle doodle. Each has a life of its own, each has a power and a beauty all of its own. Some you will throw away, but if you are anything like me, there are some that you keep and treasure and come back to time after time."

This was so cool. I was nodding like mad. It was like she *knew* me. It was like she knew I had a hiding place for all my special pictures. This was weird, but in a good way.

"Go on, take a look. I don't mind."

She was smiling at me, as if she could feel my excitement. Hugo woofed as I bent down and started to flick slowly through the pictures.

I looked at picture after picture of fiery reds and ambers and angry blacks and sunshine yellows. I picked up one and found myself staring into big black beautiful eyes belonging to dragons and snakes floating amongst spirals of plants and trees. I traced over the branches and it was almost like I could feel Margaret as she painted it. Too weird. I put the picture down and stood up. Margaret looked pleased.

"You can have that one if you like."
"Really?"

She laughed.

"Yes, really. A gift from me and Hugo."

I bent down and picked it up. I loved it already.

"Thank you."

I skipped back up the road towards home, holding onto the picture tight, so it wouldn't fly away in the wind. When I got in, Dad was in the kitchen and Gran was in the lounge. No idea where Lou was. Upstairs probably. Mum was at work.

"Hey Dad, look what Margaret gave me!"

Dad stopped peeling potatoes to look at my picture.

"That's beautiful. Very intricate. Did she really give it to you?"

"Yeah, of course she did."

Duh. How else would I have it? I'd never take it without asking.

"Wow. That's really nice of her. I didn't realise she was an artist."

"Nor did I. She's got this painting den and there's paint everywhere and pictures stacked up against the wall. She says she has a whole room of pictures upstairs too. It was amazing and she was telling me all about how it feels to paint and how she loses herself in her paintings. I want to be an artist when I grow up."

I still wanted to be a children's book illustrator like Quentin Blake but I could do both.

"Well maybe you could do some painting with her one day and she could teach you some of her techniques."

"Do you think she would?"

"Well, she might. You don't know if you don't ask."

I thought about it for a moment. It would be cool to work with a real artist, but then there was something nice about the fact that she wasn't a teacher and we could just chat and play with Hugo. I wasn't so sure. Maybe. Maybe when I was a bit older. I liked doing my own stuff anyway.

"Maybe. I'm going to go and put this picture up by my bed now."

"OK. Maybe we could get a frame for it at the weekend."

"Awesome! Thanks Dad."

I ran upstairs and stuck the picture next to my bed with some Blutack. I considered having a quick read of Lou's diary, but thought that might spoil my mood, so I didn't. I went back downstairs to see what Gran was up to instead.

I pushed open the lounge door, but it was stuck. I pushed a bit harder, but it would only open a tiny bit. Gran appeared from behind the door and handed me a piece of paper and grasped my hand when I took it from her.

"Go and give it to them."

"To who? What is it?"

"They'll understand. You have to get help."

She was whispering and peering round me, trying to see Dad, I guess. I opened up the piece of paper, but there was just a load of squiggles and random marks on it. Almost like one of Margaret's pictures on her walls but not nearly as good, obviously.

"I don't understand, Gran. What is it?"

"It's a note; you need to give it to them. They'll get us out of here."

"What's up, Katie?"

Dad had come to see what was going on.

"Um.. Gran gave me this note to give to somebody."

I turned round and pulled a face at him, trying to tell him that Gran had gone weird again. He looked at the note and raised his eyebrows at me.

"Don't show *him*. *He* mustn't read it. Oh, what have you done? You stupid child!"

Gran slammed the door. She'd never shouted at me before. We were friends. Dad tried to open the door and had to use all his weight just to open it a bit.

"Vera? Vera, come on out of there, or at least open the door."

"I'm NOT coming. You can't make me. You and *her.*"

It was like she spat out *"her"*. It was making me feel really uncomfortable, hot and prickly, like I could feel Mr. Nobody in the room. I shivered and backed away behind Dad who was still trying to force the door open. I could just about see Gran, who looked like she was pushing an armchair against the door. Surely Dad was stronger than Gran? But then maybe Gran had help. Mr. Nobody kind of help. I shook my head; this was just getting silly now.

Dad paused and so did Gran. It was like it was a truce. What was that thing in the First World War we'd learned last term? The soldiers on both sides of the Front had stopped for Christmas and played a game of football. I couldn't really see Dad and Gran playing football. Dad hated football anyway. Said he was lucky he had daughters.

Gran was panting. Must have been hard work, pushing the chair against the door. I noticed then how odd she looked, like she hadn't really thought about how to get dressed properly this morning. She had her bra on top of her jumper *again*, her hair was all sticking up, she had her skirt on back to front and her stockings rolled down to her ankles, revealing her lumpy blue veins which criss-crossed her legs like the blue lines on smelly cheese. She peered at us through her thick glasses and then said,

"I'm not coming out, you know. And you're not coming in."

"Come on Vera, why don't I make you a nice cup of tea?"

"Return to sender,
address unknown.
No such number,
no such zone."

Oh no. Gran was singing Elvis again. But she was singing it at us, like she was trying to hurt us with the words.

"Come on, don't be daft."

"NO SUCH NUMBER,
NO SUCH ZONE."

She was shouting it out now. I tugged at Dad's sleeve.

"Come on Dad, let's just leave her alone. I don't think she wants to come out.

"She doesn't. That's what's so bloody ridiculous."

I pretended I hadn't heard him swear. Sometimes it was just best to leave Gran alone. She was like a goldfish anyway. Or that's what

Molly said. She said that goldfish forget stuff all the time so that the next time they swim round their bowl it's all exciting and new again. Made sense otherwise they'd die of boredom. It meant that Gran would forget and come out soon if we left her alone.

"Come on Dad, leave her alone. She will come out eventually. I bet she comes out for tea."

"Oh damn!"

Dad ran into the kitchen – he must have forgotten about something cooking.

I looked back to the lounge door. Gran was quiet. The door was ajar and just visible through the crack was a slice of my gran: she looked scared. Then the slice of Gran spoke.

"I'm not coming out. You can't make me, you know."

The door slammed shut and she disappeared.

And Dad thought I should invite Molly over to play. No way.

18

Vera remembers Pete

Vera

Vera wrote on her piece of paper. It was taking her forever.

Come on, get those words out.

"I am. Will you stop nagging?"

Well I can't read your writing, can you?

Vera stopped and picked up the piece of paper, holding it close to her eyes. Too fuzzy. No she couldn't read it, but that didn't mean the milkman wouldn't be able to. She picked up the pen and laboriously started to write again. She had to get the words out. If the milkman read it, he would be sure to send a rescue party for her. She would slip it in the bottle and then, when they put it outside, he would get it. She smiled at her ingenuity.

You are SO slow. He'll have come and gone before you've finished.

"Oh, do be quiet."

Vera looked up annoyed but, to her surprise, the room was empty. He'd been talking to her just a minute ago and there was something familiar about that voice, after all. She'd thought for a while that she recognised it, that maybe Mr. Nobody was a Mr. Somebody. She started humming to herself as she rolled up the note into a tiny, tight cylinder. The humming grew louder and she found the words,

"Only the lonely,
know the way I feel tonight.
Only the lonely,
know this feeling ain't right.
Only the lonely,
know the heartaches I've been through.
Only the lonely,
know I cried and cried only for you."

Pete! Her lovely Pete. She was crying for Pete. It had been his voice she had heard, it must have been. Where had he gone? Forgetting about the note she was writing for the milkman, she dropped it onto the table and walked quickly to the front door. She turned the doorknob but it didn't work. She turned it again the other way and pulled the handle down with her other hand. It took her several attempts, but at last she had it open. She wasn't so sure now. She peered outside and didn't see anything familiar. She stood for a moment, rubbing her hands together against the cold. It really was very cold.

She had to go. Pete would expect her to find him. She had to pull herself together. She'd go uphill. If you go up, you always have to go down eventually. She set off at a brisk pace to keep warm, ignoring the front door, which was banging against the wall in the wind. She put her head down, defying the wind and battled on. Pete would be waiting for her.

19

An unwelcome visitor at school

Katie

I hated maths. Especially when we just had to sit there doing worksheets while Mr. Braithwaite did his marking. *Bor-ring.* Ten minutes to go and then we could go home.

I stretched back and yawned and as I did so, I looked out of the window. We were on the top floor, looking out over the front of the school and the smooth bit of playground. The bit of playground round the side of the school had bits that were rough and broken and there were tree stumps around the place. I expect they wanted the front to look smart for the parents. That's where we did our skipping anyway.

I'd been rocking back on my chair but then I saw her and it made me stop suddenly and crash back down. I wish I hadn't, because the class was so quiet it startled everyone and Mr. Braithwaite glared at me. I put my head right down and ignored what I'd seen.

"Hey, look! There's an old weirdo in our playground."

That was Carys' voice. I suddenly found my maths *really* interesting.

"Where? Let me see."

"It must be somebody's gran."

"What, dressed like that? No way."

"She's well weird. Look, everyone's walking away from her."

"Settle down everyone. You have five minutes to go and I want to see those sheets completed."

Mr. Braithwaite got up and wandered over to the window. I risked raising my head and regretted it immediately because I looked straight into Carys's eyes – she sat next to the window. She grinned at me. Mr. Braithwaite was standing next to her, looking out. Gran was in the playground, which shouldn't be odd really, because there were lots of mums and dads there to pick up their kids. The thing is, the mums and dads were standing in groups mostly and my gran was going from group to group and people were actually backing away from her and shaking their heads. I really felt sorry for Gran.

People could be so mean, but I wasn't going to admit she was my gran. The trouble was the way she was dressed.

She'd done her usual trick of wearing her bra on top of her jumper, but not just a jumper, she had a cardigan on too and the bra was on top of that. It must be really uncomfortable. She was wearing Lou's baseball cap (Lou would go mad when she found out) and she looked like she had pyjama trousers on. Of course she had her slippers on too. Everyone else out there was in coats, hats and gloves because it was end of November and it was freezing.

Mrs. Tavistock, the school secretary, was outside now and trying to get her to come indoors, but it looked like she was refusing. Good. Maybe she'd wander off. I didn't mean that in a mean way, I just meant I wish she wasn't here, at school, being weird. I wished she could just be Gran again.

"That's Katie's gran."

Carys was speaking to Mr. Braithwaite and was looking all worried but I knew she was faking it.

"Do you think you ought to let Katie go and get her? I mean, she must be really cold dressed like that."

She turned to me with her fake smile. Big fat idiot.

"That's right isn't it, Katie? It's your gran. My mum says there's something wrong with her brain. Is that right, Katie?"

Other kids in my class were trying to look now and some were laughing. I'd gone bright red again and I could almost feel Mr. Nobody laughing behind me. I wanted to get up and defend Gran from them all, but I kind of didn't want to either. Any minute now, Gran would probably start singing Elvis and that would just do it. I'd never be able to come to school again. Mr. Braithwaite turned to me.

"Is that right, Katie? Is that your gran?"

I nodded. More kids were laughing now. Mr. Braithwaite snapped at them.

"That's enough! Back to your seats everyone. I have NOT said it's the end of class. Katie, perhaps you'd better go down and help your gran. Take your things with you."

I nodded, picked up my stuff and left via the cloakroom to get my coat, hat and gloves. I put them all on. I didn't want everyone thinking I was weird like Gran.

Some of the other classes were coming out of school when I got downstairs and I almost thought of keeping my head down and getting lost in the crowd, but I couldn't do it. Gran needed me. I walked over to Mrs. Tavistock who had her arm around my gran's shoulders.

"Hi, Gran."

"Oh, Lisa, thank goodness you're here."

Gran shook off Mrs. Tavistock and embraced me. I just knew Carys would be watching. I'd never live it down, but then I remembered it was Saturday tomorrow, so I wouldn't have to see her again until Monday. Mrs. Tavistock was looking at me strangely, either because she couldn't believe I was related to this weirdo, or because Gran had used my mum's name instead of mine.

"Gran, it's me, Katie."

Gran looked at me like I was stupid.

"Of course it is dear. Shall we go now?"

"Er…OK."

I hooked my arm into Gran's and looked at Mrs. Tavistock who was in the way.

"Katie, would you not rather wait for your mum?"

"Nah, it's OK."

"Well your gran seems very distressed. I'm not sure you should take her home by yourself."

"It's OK. We'll go straight home."

"It's not that Katie, it's just that I think it would be better if your mum or dad came to collect you. Why don't you both come in and I'll give your parents a call?"

I just wanted to get out of school before even more people came to gawp at us.

"Really, we're fine. Aren't we, Gran?"

Gran nodded and smiled at Mrs. Tavistock.

"Oh yes we are, thank you very much. So lovely to have met you. Off we go, Lisa. Time to make your tea."

Gran and I started to walk, leaving Mrs. Tavistock staring after us, probably wondering who Lisa was. Gran didn't walk fast these days, so it took us ages to get out of the playground, especially because Gran kept stopping and smiling and saying hello to people. I'd just got to the school gates when Molly appeared, breathless.

"Hey!"

"Hey, Molly."

"I ran all the way from the cloakroom. Are you OK?"

"Yeah, we're fine. Just need to get home."

"My mum's just over there, look. Do you want a lift?"

"Nah, it's OK thanks."

Though maybe it wasn't OK. Gran had stopped and was laughing at somebody's dad, I swear she was. Molly looked from Gran to me and looked like she didn't know whether to laugh or stay serious. It was actually pretty funny. The dad of somebody in Year One was really short and had a massive bum and he'd just tripped over his dog lead backwards and landed splat on his bum, like it was a giant inflatable

133

cushion.

"Oh, would you look at that!" my gran exclaimed.

We did, and both Molly and I smiled, but we didn't laugh, not like Gran who seemed to think it was hilarious. This is Gran, who didn't appear to know that she was wearing her bra on top of her jumper, her pyjama bottoms and her slippers.

The thing I liked about Gran was that she didn't care what people thought any more, she just said and did what she wanted to. I envied her that, but it could be really embarrassing. Like now.

"Come on, Gran, let's go."

"Oh the poor man. Lucky he's got a big bottom."

Molly's hand flew to her mouth to cover up her laugh. I would have laughed, but I think the man had heard. His son certainly had. Think he was called Jamie, I didn't know him. He started to shout at us.

"Don't you laugh at my dad, you silly old cow. Why've you come out in your bra anyway? Loser!"

His dad told him off and tried to yank him away, but he was looking at us over his shoulder.

"Well, what a rude child!"

I loved Gran. I mean I would have been embarrassed if I were her, but not Gran, she didn't care. I did care though, and it was time to go.

"All women wear bras, didn't you know that?" Molly shouted after him and he stuck his tongue out.

In the end, I let Molly and her mum give us a lift home. Mrs. Tavistock was still hovering so I thought it would be best just to go. Of course it wasn't easy because Gran wanted to know who Molly was and what her mum was doing and it took ages to get her into the car. She started fiddling in her pockets when she got into the car and didn't listen to Molly's mum, who had to lean across her to get the seatbelt and fasten her in. I rolled my eyes at Molly. Gran was *such* hard work.

Molly's mum dropped us off right outside our house. The door was wide open which was odd. Molly's mum thought it was because Mum had come home but Mum wasn't supposed to be home until later. We got Gran out of the car, but then of course she didn't want to go in.

"I must find him."

"Who, Gran?"

"Pete. I must find Pete."

"I don't know who you mean, Gran."

"Oh, of course you do. My Pete."

"Oh, you mean Granddad Pete? He's dead, Gran. He died ages ago."

I probably shouldn't have said it like that. I mean, imagine not knowing your husband is dead and then suddenly someone tells you he is. If it had been me I bet I would have burst into tears, but not Gran. She looked at me and for a few seconds it was like she was really looking at me, like it was my old gran back behind her eyes, like she *knew*. Like she knew that she'd been taken over somehow by this weirdo gran, by Mr. Nobody, and her eyes looked all watery like she might cry. It was cold though, so it might have been the wind. Then she got her eyes back, the ones that always looked a bit confused and now they looked properly confused.

"Come on, Gran, let's go in and have a hot drink. It's freezing out here."

And she let me take her inside. I'd forgotten about Molly and her mum who both followed us in. Molly's mum shut the door behind her.

"Is your mum in?"

I shrugged.

"I don't think so."

"Well someone must be; your door was open."

I called out, but no one answered. I put the kettle on while Molly's mum checked through the house. Molly was my best friend, but it didn't mean that her mum could just go through our house. I could guess what had happened; Gran would have left the door open when she went out. I tried to explain that to Molly's mum, but she insisted on checking that everything was OK.

I made Gran a cup of tea and opened the biscuit tin. At least she hadn't eaten them all again. She didn't drink her tea though, she went into the lounge and shut the door and I could hear her moving the armchair against it again. That always made Dad really cross. Good job he wasn't here.

"My mum never lets me make cups of tea."

Molly whispered it to me because her mum was on her phone calling my mum. I hadn't asked her to. My mum never used to let me make tea either, but that all changed when Gran moved in. I guess she realised that Gran was more dangerous than I was.

"What are these?"

Molly had found some tightly rolled up pieces of paper on the table and she was unravelling one of them.

"I dunno."

I looked over her shoulder and recognised Gran's squiggles from the time she had given me a note to give to somebody. I wasn't going to tell Molly that though, even if she was my best friend. It wasn't fair on Gran somehow.

"Oh, it's just some rubbish."

I grabbed it from her and the other bits of

paper on the table and threw them all in the bin.

I wish Gran hadn't come to school that day. Not just because everyone saw how weird she was, but also because it meant I now had to go to After School Club every day, apart from when I went to Molly's. Molly's mum had told my mum what had happened and school had rung too and Mum said I couldn't be at home alone with Gran any more, because it wasn't fair on me. What wasn't fair was making me go to After School Club and anyway, surely it was better if I was at home looking after Gran, so she couldn't do anything stupid. But Mum said that Gran wasn't my responsibility. She hadn't minded that the day before.

That night I had another Mr. Nobody nightmare. He was at school and doing the assembly and he'd made me come up in front of everyone, but I was only wearing my knickers and the whole school laughed at me. When I woke up, I could still hear the laughter in my ears and the sheet was all damp. I thought I'd wet myself, but it was only sweat. I got up, even though it was still dark, because my pyjamas were all wet too, but when I got out of bed I was frozen. Lou wasn't in bed. I pulled my dressing gown on and opened the door, being extra careful to step over the creaky floorboard. I crept downstairs to the landing and heard muffled voices coming up the stairs. I crept down further and sat a few steps up from the bottom, where I could hear better. Mum was crying.

"We're doing the right thing, Lisa. We've looked after her as best we can, but it's affecting the kids too much. It's affecting all of us. And the stress is no good for Gran either, is it?"

"Katie keeps having nightmares, Mum."

That was my business. I should be the one telling Mum. I got up and went down the last few steps to tell her myself, but it was like I'd walked slap into a glass wall.

I just stopped dead. Lou was standing up and trying to cuddle Mum like *she* was the mum and Dad was sitting next to mum holding her hand. Mum's other hand was holding Lou's arm and she had her eyes shut. I got that rubbed out feeling again, only this time it felt like someone was scrubbing really hard at my pencil outline and they wouldn't stop. I wished Lou would go back to mean and moody Lou, I wished Mum would talk to *me* and I wished Dad would notice me and come and comfort *me*. More than anything, I wished Gran and Mr. Nobody would just go away.

I ran upstairs. I didn't care if they heard me. It wasn't like they cared anyway. I got my pencils out and my torch and hid under the covers, drawing. It was a family of four but the fourth one was barely there, just a faint outline at the edge of the page.

20

No one tells me what's really going on

Katie

It was the weekend. No Carys and no maths. I was going to Molly's house today. Dad had arranged it and told me at breakfast.

Gran said she was going to her friend's house too and everyone ignored her. I hadn't thought about Gran having real friends. She was always getting ready to meet her pretend friends, or maybe they were friends who were dead, because Gran was pretty old. Lou said she was 78. I always helped her to get ready and Mum said I shouldn't encourage her, but I figured it couldn't be much fun being Gran in our house, so I didn't see why she couldn't at least have some pretend fun.

I didn't help her this morning though. I was

looking forward to getting out of the house that I didn't belong in any more.

It was only when Dad dropped me off that I realised he wanted me out of the way.

"Have a good day, Katie."

Then he looked over my head to Molly's mum. I wished I wasn't so small for my age.

"Thank you *so* much."

"Oh, don't be silly. It's the least I can do for you all. Good luck."

"Thanks. Be good, pumpkin."

"Why did she say 'good luck', Dad?"

He glanced back at Molly's mum.

"Oh, it doesn't matter. Have fun."

He ruffled my hair. I glared at him. He was up to something and he knew that I knew, because he didn't tell me off for glaring. He just got back in the car, waved and drove off. I asked Molly's mum, who was pushing me into the house.

"Why did you say 'good luck' to my dad?"

"Oh, I don't know. I guess I thought you could all do with some luck. It's been a bit tough recently with your gran, hasn't it? Now, what are you two girls going to do all day?"

Adults always do that when they don't want to answer your question, they speak really quickly and think they're being so clever at distracting you. I wanted to get out. I didn't want to stay in their house.

"Shall we go to the allotments, Molly? We could build the den."

"Yeah, great idea. Can we, Mum?"

Molly's mum didn't look sure. She was a bit dainty really to approve of den building but Molly wasn't.

"Pleeease, Mum? And can we take a picnic?"

Molly's mum frowned.

"Well I suppose you can take a snack with you. It's too cold for a picnic. I want you both back here for lunch. OK?"

"OK, Mum. Can we have some chocolate?"

"You can go and help yourselves to a snack. And Molly, I want you to wear your watch so you know when to come home. I want you back here by 12. OK?"

"OK, Mum."

Molly grabbed my arm and rushed into the kitchen with me. We got a Kit Kat, a bag of Hula Hoops and a carton of apple juice each.

It was freezing up at the allotments. I wished I had Dad's key to the shed, but instead we sat in the hedge (it was a useless den) and ate all our snack in one go. We were still cold.

"Let's go into the woods."

I wasn't sure. I still had bad memories of the last time.

"C'mon. It'll be fun."

143

Molly was already pushing her way out of the hedge onto the wood side. I followed.

"I'll race you up the hill. Come on."

Molly was running and shouting at me so I started to run too. It was ace. I loved running. I was the fastest girl in my year and I soon caught up with Molly. We got to the top of the hill together and collapsed at the top, panting and laughing. I jumped up when I'd got my breath back and started to run back down.

"Come on, let's do it again!"

I don't know how many times we did it, but we got so hot we piled up our coats, hats and gloves at the top of the hill. We were lying on top of our clothes laughing when we heard voices. Molly recognised them first.

"It's Carys and Anna."

I turned to look and I could see them coming down the path towards us. My heart was thudding and it wasn't because I'd been running.

"C'mon on Katie, let's go."

But I didn't want to. It would look like we were running away. I picked my stuff up.

"Oh, look who it is, Anna."

They stopped in front of us.

"Playing in the woods, are you? You're such a baby, Katie."

Carys sneered at me, but this time I wasn't going to let her speak to me like that.

"What are *you* doing in the woods then?"

"We're walking, aren't we Anna?"

"Oh really? Where to?"

"None of your business, Katie. How's your gran today? Gone out in her bra and slippers again?"

She sniggered and Anna laughed. Anna didn't have a mind of her own any more. It was like she'd been possessed by Carys. I felt sorry for her.

"C'mon on, Katie. They're not worth it."

Molly was trying to pull me away. Carys smiled at her, with that smile that means she hates you.

"I don't know why you hang out with her, Molly."

"She's my friend and I'll hang out with who I want to."

Molly was the *best,* best friend and she made me feel braver than I had in ages.

"Come on Molly, we don't want to hang out with these losers."

I grinned at them both, feeling cool and turned away. Something whacked me on the head and I ducked, too late.

"Ouch!"

I turned round and this time a stick hit me right in the face, just under my eye. It stung.

"Hey! Stop it, you idiot!"

"Yeah? Why should I?"

Carys bent down to pick up another stick. Anna was backing away from her and suddenly looking very guilty. Molly was trying to pull me away again.

"Carys, there's someone coming. Let's go."

I turned round to see who Anna meant and the next thing I knew Hugo was bounding up to me, tail wagging. He started barking and jumping around me in circles, all excited. I bent down to make a fuss of him and I heard Margaret coming up behind us.

"Hello girls."

"Hi, Margaret."

Hugo was still excited and trying to lick my nose. Molly was nervous of dogs so she'd backed away and Carys and Anna had started to run off down the path.

"Clever Hugo. Who's a clever dog?"

I buried my face in his neck and he licked my ear.

"It's OK dear, he's just excited to see Katie again. He won't hurt you."

Molly came a bit closer, but flinched whenever Hugo went near her so Margaret put his lead on. I stood up.

"Have you been in the wars again, Katie?"

I touched my face where the stick had hit me. It was sore and felt bumpy.

"Carys threw a stick at her."

Margaret looked horrified.

"Really?"

I nodded.

"Yeah. She's the one I was telling you about. She's always mean to me."

Molly nodded.

"It's true. She's really horrible. And so's Anna. She used to be nice, but not now that she's friends with Carys."

"I thought I recognised the other little girl. Is that Anna Peacock?"

I nodded.

"Well I know her mum. We go to choir together."

I never knew Margaret went to a choir. I didn't know any grown-up who went to a choir.

"I shouldn't think she'd be very happy to know her daughter's mixing with a girl like that. I might have a word. Look at the state of your face."

I touched my face again. It had started to throb.

When Molly's mum dropped me off home later in the afternoon, I could tell they'd all been somewhere together. I just knew. Mum did at least ask what I'd done to my face. I told her what I'd told Molly's mum, that I'd tripped over and caught it on a tree root. What was the point of telling her the truth? I could tell she didn't really want to know. She'd asked me, but she'd been looking at Gran who seemed to think she was in a hotel or something. That always made Mum stressed. She should just let Gran imagine what she wanted to. It was a lot easier.

"Where's that man gone?"

Mum looked really tired.

"If you mean where is Gary, Mum, then he's upstairs cleaning up."

"Oh, that's alright then. It does seem better than that other place, doesn't it?"

I watched as Lou looked at Mum and raised her eyebrows and Mum looked at Gran like she was trying to work out what to say. I wondered what Dad was cleaning up anyway, then I had a horrible thought. What if she had done another poo in my wardrobe?

"I'm not sure I know what you mean, Mum?"

"Oh come on, you know exactly what I mean!"

The trouble is we never really did and then Gran wouldn't remember either which meant she'd get upset and Mum and Dad would get annoyed with her. They should just leave her alone. I decided I would show them how to handle Gran.

"I know what you mean, Gran."

Lou gave me a Look. I ignored her. It was her 'You're So Stupid' Look.

Gran beamed at me.

"It's really so much better here, isn't it?"

"Yes it is, Gran."

Then Mum gave me a Look too, a confused look. I shrugged at her and carried on talking to Gran. Maybe *she* would tell me where they'd all been today.

"Have you been out today, Gran?"

"Oh yes, we have – to a marvellous establishment. I didn't think much of *him* though."

"Who?"

"Him upstairs."

Gran seemed to have a thing about Dad.

"Oh I like him, Gran."

She looked surprised.

"Do you? Well I don't. I don't trust him. Not one inch."

"I don't see why not. He's clearing up your mess, Gran."

That was from Lou, who was giving Gran the Look now. I was kind of glad because then Mum would see what she was really like again. I wanted to know what Dad was clearing up, so I walked past Gran to the stairs and caught a whiff of something not very nice. Kind of compost-like.

That was another thing Gran was doing now: refusing to wash. I'd heard Mum try to get her into the bath and getting cross with her. I don't think she'd had a bath for a whole week. I can't believe they'd taken her out with them somewhere today, smelling like that.

I ran upstairs into my old room, where Dad was. He had rubber gloves on and he was picking up bits of glass.

"What happened, Dad?"

"Oh, your gran dropped a glass and it smashed."

I didn't think things smashed if you dropped them on carpet. At least it wasn't poo again. Then I saw the big wet stain on the wall. She must have thrown something against the wall and whatever it was had smashed onto the carpet. But why would Dad lie to me? Why wouldn't anyone tell me what was going on?

I left Dad to it and went on upstairs to Lou's room, which I had all to myself for once. I was still burning to read her diary again, but didn't dare in case she came upstairs. Instead, I got my pencils out and stared at Margaret's picture on the wall for inspiration. Then I started to doodle. It wasn't anything really, at least I wasn't thinking as I was doing it. It started off as a flowery sort of pattern. Then the flowers turned into beanstalks and they came out of a steaming compost heap. Hidden in the compost were two cherry red eyes. Mr. Nobody wouldn't leave me alone.

21

Gran accuses Mum and Dad

Katie

"Come on now, Mum, you need to take these."

"Get away from me. Stay away!"

"Don't be daft. Come on. You just need to take this little yellow one and the pink one. Doctor's orders."

"Whose doctor? You're lying. I haven't been to the doctor's."

"Yes, you have. I was with you."

"Nonsense. You haven't been anywhere with me. I am NOT taking them."

Gran's voice was getting louder. I peeked over the banisters but couldn't see them. I tiptoed a few steps lower until I could just see Mum. This had happened every night this week. Mum tried to get Gran to take her pills. Gran refused. Mum tried again and Gran gave in. Gran wasn't giving in tonight, though. I went down another step and craned my head around the banisters so I could just see Gran standing with her back against the wall.

"You can't force me. You can't."

"I am not trying to force you I am helping you."

Mum's voice sounded strained. I knew that voice. She was going to explode soon.

> "Granny was in the kitchen,
> doing a bit of stitching,
> when in came the bogie man
> and pushed her *out*."

Gran's voice was high and quivering, like it was balanced on a high wire and might fall off. All the time she sang, she kept her eyes on Mum.

"You keep away from me. I know what you want."

"Really? Well if you know, then come and take these pills. They'll help you."

Mum moved round the kitchen table towards her. Gran moved away back round the other side of the table.

"For goodness sake, Mum. Will you please take these flipping pills!"

"I will NOT."

She stood there with her arms folded across her chest, shaking her head. Really, some days it was just like having an overgrown toddler in the house. That's what Dad said. He was out. He was out a lot these days.

"Please Mum, you *have* to take them."

Mum sounded fed up now.

"I do not and I will not. You're NOT going to do it. Oh no. I know what you're up to."

Gran smiled like she'd just proved something. She looked very proud of herself. I looked at Mum. She was frowning.

"What do you mean, 'up to'?"

"You know very well what I mean."

Gran nodded proudly again. I felt for Mum. It was one of those conversations that had no end. She had a lot of those with Gran.

Just then the door opened and Dad walked in. Both Mum and Gran stared at him. I thought Mum looked relieved, but Gran didn't. She looked scared. I could tell by the way her eyes got wider. She looked from him to Mum and back again. Suddenly she started shouting.

"It's HIM. He's MADE you do it. He's EVIL. Get him out of here. I told you it was him."

She said that last bit to the wall behind her. I guess she thought Mr. Nobody was there. I couldn't feel him yet, though. Sometimes I could, like all the air in the room had got heavier.

Mum tried to put her arms round Gran to calm her down, but Gran pushed her away and screamed even louder.

"GET OFF ME! GET OFF ME! I'M NOT DOING IT!"

Mum shouted back.

"I'M NOT DOING ANYTHING! And nor is Gary. Keep your voice down, will you? And Gary, for pity's sake, shut the door. We don't want everyone hearing."

Too late for that. If we could hear next door going up their stairs, I was pretty sure they could hear Gran screaming – with or without the front door shut. Dad shut it, though. And then he tried to help. Sort of.

He walked quickly over to Gran and stepped in between her and Mum. Gran put her arms in front of her face and she screamed again.

"NO! DON'T HIT ME! LEAVE ME ALONE!"

"Will you be quiet! No one is trying to hit you. Just everyone calm down."

Gran was trembling now but she spoke more quietly.

"Please, please don't hurt me. Please leave me alone."

She backed away to the wall. I wanted to run down the stairs and shout at her that Dad wouldn't hurt anyone. I couldn't understand why she would say that.

"Gary, I think you'd better leave. I don't think you're helping."

Dad turned round to look at Mum.

"You want me to leave my own home while your mother accuses me, as loudly as she can, of trying to hurt her? Fine! I'm sorry I came home."

He pushed past Mum and went out, slamming the front door behind him. It felt like he'd taken some of the air out of the room with him. I wish he hadn't done that, because I was beginning to not feel very well.

Mum pulled her hands through her hair and looked like she was about to say something, but changed her mind. Instead she sat down at the table. Gran was still going on.

"Don't you think that just because *he's* gone, that I don't think you'll try again. I won't let you."

Gran was glaring at Mum.

"What exactly do you think I'm trying to do?"

"I don't think. I *know*."

Gran was running her tongue around her front teeth and nodding her head like she'd just worked out something she wasn't supposed to know.

Mum sighed.

"Come on then. Tell me. What *do* you think is going on?"

She raised her eyebrows at Gran like she did with Lou when she was annoyed with her. She should just leave her alone. Why had no one else in this family worked it out yet? Gran always got worse, the more you tried to show her she was wrong.

"You must think I'm stupid, but it's OK. I've told them."

Gran looked disgusted as she said this, like Mum had really offended her.

"Told who what?"

"The police, of course."

She paused and then she delivered her punch line.

"I told them that you are trying to poison me. That you want me dead. You and that man. They'll be here any minute. Then you'll be sorry."

"You've done *what*?"

"You heard. I called the police. I told them everything. They were lovely. You can't get away with it."

I didn't think she could have done, because she couldn't work the phone any more. But what if she had managed it? Gran had really gone mental this time. There was no way Mum and Dad would poison her. Why would she think that? But what if the police believed her? What if they took Mum away to the station to question her? I wished Dad was here to sort it out. I

157

started to feel really scared that it was all getting out of control. I squeezed my eyes tight shut, but I could see cherry red pinpricks, thousands of them. The air felt heavy, like I couldn't breathe. Mr. Nobody was back. Then I felt Lou run down the stairs past me.

"How DARE you? You stupid old woman. Mum is looking after you. Don't you get it? If it wasn't for Mum, you'd be in some mental home for old people. Why did you have to go and do a stupid thing like call the police? You're mad. You're wrecking this family. I wish you'd just get on and DIE."

Lou screamed that last word and then there was silence. I don't think anyone knew what to say. I was sure someone would hear my heart thumping against my ribs. It felt and sounded like a runaway train clattering over the tracks. I tried to quietly take a few deep breaths to calm it down before someone heard it.

Gran smiled, like she'd been proved right about something, but then she saw me and her eyes did that thing where they go clear and she looks at me properly. I looked back and I could see that she was scared. I wanted to go and give her a hug, even though she'd said all those horrible things. It wasn't her, it was Mr. Nobody and someone needed to rescue her. I got up and spoke softly, like Margaret does to Hugo.

"It's OK, Gran. Lou didn't mean it."

"I did."

Mum got up.

"OK, that's enough. Lou, you're not helping."

I led Gran to a chair and helped her sit down. She looked like she hadn't a clue what was going on. I really did feel sorry for her, but there was something else that was filling my insides up and making them fizz like a sherbet dip: Mum had told Lou off and *I* was the one who had calmed Gran down.

"Where's Dad gone?"

How could I have forgotten about Dad? I looked over to Mum. Her eyes were full of tears and before I could do anything, Lou had gone over and put her arms round her. Lou was taller than Mum now. I was still a midget. That's what Lou always said. I didn't feel fizzy inside any more; I felt carved out and strangely empty like a pumpkin that wants its seeds back. Dad used to call me pumpkin. Still does sometimes.

I watched Mum and Lou. I wanted to hold Mum and I wanted her to hold me and say it was all going to be OK. My family was all mixed up. I shouldn't be comforting Gran (and actually, now I remembered what she'd said, I didn't want to comfort her any more), Lou shouldn't be looking after Mum, and Dad shouldn't have just gone out. I started to cry.

"There there, dear."

Gran was stroking my arm so I moved away. It was all her fault. I didn't want her comfort. I couldn't stop crying but I had nowhere to go. Mum saw me and pushed Lou away, beckoning me to come to her. She had tears down her face too. I sat on her lap and buried my head in her chest and cried and cried. She smelt of washing powder and supper and mum. She hugged me tight. The front door opened and shut and I heard Dad, but I didn't look up. I felt him kiss me on the top of my head.

"I'm sorry, Lisa."

Mum didn't say anything but I felt Dad's arms around us. I didn't know where Lou and Gran were, and I didn't care.

22

Mum won't talk to me properly

Katie

I hadn't done my poem yet for Mrs. Jackson, but I had been thinking about it. It had to be about Gran, really. I was sitting at the dining table chewing the end of my pencil, wondering how to start it. I couldn't do it in our bedroom, because Lou was always there now. She'd finished with Max. Apparently, he was "too immature". Shame, I liked Max. Mum was cooking and Gran was watching telly I think. Dad had a staff meeting tonight, so he'd be back late. I liked it just being me and Mum, like it sometimes used to be, before Gran came.

"Mum?"

"Hmmm?"

"I've got to write a poem."

"OK."

Mum was putting a pie in the oven. She wasn't really listening, I could tell.

"It's about someone close to me."

"Hmmmm."

"MUM!"

Mum looked surprised, like I hadn't actually been trying to talk to her for ages.

"What?"

"I said: I've got to write a poem about someone close to me."

"I know, I heard you."

"Oh, well it didn't sound like you did."

"Katie, I was busy. So, who are you going to write it about then?"

"Gran, I think."

"Sounds like a good idea."

"Does it?"

"Well yes, why do you ask?"

"Just thought you might not like it."

Mum was frowning at me.

"Why wouldn't I?"

"Well, you know."

"No, I don't. Tell me."

"Well, she's a bit weird, isn't she? And I'd kind of have to describe that in the poem. Mrs. Jackson says we have to describe how they make us cross or happy."

"Well, she's probably the perfect choice

then."

"What would you say about her?"

"Oh, I don't know. It's your poem, you need to work out what *you* feel."

So annoying. I wanted Mum to *talk* to me, not write my poem. She never talked to me about Gran.

"No, I mean what makes you happy and sad about Gran? I don't mean write my poem for me. I just wondered what you think, that's all."

Mum came and sat down next to me. I waited. She looked at me and chewed her top lip, like she was thinking what she could tell me.

"I won't tell anyone. It's just between you and me."

Well, I might tell Margaret, or Molly maybe, but no one else. Mum smiled at me.

"Well, I think what makes me happy is when I hear her singing and humming, because it reminds me a bit of what she used to be like, before she became ill."

"Yeah, I like that too. It's funny when she sings Elvis, but not funny when she sings those other weird songs."

"You mean those old playground songs? I think they were skipping songs when she was your age."

"Oh. Well, it's still a bit weird when she sings them."

Mum laughed. I wanted her to tell me about what made her sad. I wanted her to tell me what Gran did. I wanted her to know that Lou wasn't the only one who could listen.

"What about what makes you sad?"

Mum shrugged and got up.

"Oh, all sorts of things."

She started filling up the sink to do the washing up. There was only one bowl to wash, that was it.

"Like what?"

"Oh, when she forgets who we are. When she gets anxious about things or doesn't understand something. You know, you've seen her do it."

"What else?"

Mum was scrubbing the bowl really hard.

"Oh, nothing. Why don't you go and write something now? You don't need me to tell you what I think."

"I was just asking because I was interested."

"I know, Katie, but now's not really the time. Can't you see I'm busy?"

It never was the right time, unless she was talking to Lou, of course. She hadn't even asked me how I felt about Gran. She should be interested. I might as well not bother being in this family any more. I didn't want to write the stupid poem. I was going to draw a picture instead.

It was a puff of smoke with my eyes and hair and it was coming out of a cigar smoked by Mr. Nobody. Mum, Dad and Lou were holding hands, watching telly. Only Gran was looking at me but she couldn't see me, because her eyes had shutters on them, like on a window. My puff of smoke was floating away. By the time I'd finished drawing, it was teatime. I'd have to do the poem tomorrow night.

Later, when I went up to bed, I lay awake looking at Margaret's picture. There was something about the coils and tails and snakes' eyes that actually made me feel safer: like they were looking out for me. I had a feeling that it should be scary but that because Margaret had given it to me as a gift, it was only scary for other people. It was like it was protecting me, because that night I had no nightmares about Mr. Nobody. Instead, I dreamed that I was walking in the woods with Hugo and we ran and ran until we were so fast we took off and flew. We rode on the gusts of wind which carried us home to my bed, where I slept until morning with Hugo on my feet.

I woke up early with pins and needles in my feet and my poem in my head. I wrote it down quickly before I forgot it and I gave Margaret's picture a thumbs-up. I rushed my breakfast (no one noticed, of course) and then found some better words to use instead of the ones I'd woken up with. I finished it off by doing a border of snakes around it, like the snakes in Margaret's picture. They didn't have anything to do with the poem really, but it was like they'd helped me to write it and because I was going to have to read the poem out, I thought that having the snakes there would help me to do it better. They'd remind me of Hugo and Margaret. She'd told me that if I was ever scared about something, I should just shut my eyes and think of something that made me feel happy and confident and then I'd be able to handle whatever it was.

I was going to try it out in class.

23

Vera does something she shouldn't

Vera

"I shouldn't have gone away,
so I'm walking back today,
walking back to happiness.
Walking back to happiness with
you-oooo-oo-ooooo"

Vera sang happily as she pulled clothes out
of her drawers and tossed them onto the bed.

"Laid aside foolish pride,
la-la-la, la-la-la
ooo-ooo-oo-oo-oo-ooooo.
Walking back to happiness with
you-ooooo-ooo-oooo."

Soon there was a mound of knickers, bras, tights, skirts, jumpers, trousers and tops, all piled high in a jumbled heap on her bed and overflowing onto the floor.

"Goodness, what a lot of clothes we have to pack."

She sorted through the pile, making smaller jumbled up piles out of the large one.

"We need a *thing*, don't we?"

She stood next to the bed, gazing down at the mess of clothes, scratching her hand.

"It opens and shuts. You put things in it for the journey. Oh, you know what I mean."

Vera was getting agitated, her cheeks rosy with the effort of trying to remember the name of the thing she wanted.

"A, um, oh, Paddington!"

She was scratching her hand so vigorously, she didn't notice the droplets of blood falling onto the clothes from the back of her hand which had been scratched raw many times before. Someone always stuck something on the sore patch, but it got in the way so she took it off when she was alone.

"You know: 'please look after this bear.' That's it."

Vera sat down, poking at the clothes less enthusiastically now. There was the sound of a door slamming below. Vera rubbed her hand even faster, and then started scooping up the clothes and shoving them back into the drawers and under the bed. There was a knock at her door followed by a face peering round it.

"Hi, Mum. Everything OK?"

Vera nodded, still scratching. She wished she could remember the woman's name.

"Oh, no. Look at your hand."

Vera did. It was bleeding. She wiped it on her jumper.

"No, Mum. Come here, I'll sort it out for you. Come on, sit down. I'll just go and get my bag."

Vera let herself be led to the bed and she sat down, aware that she was supposed to be doing something, but she couldn't think what.

The woman who called her Mum left and came back a few moments later with her bag. She was a nurse. She didn't need a nurse.

"It's very kind of you dear, but I really don't want you to trouble yourself."

"Mum, don't be silly. It's no trouble. That needs seeing to, so it doesn't get infected."

She reached across and took Vera's hand. Vera snatched it away and held it in her other hand.

"I don't need your help. I don't need anybody's help."

She got up and started pacing round the

room. The nurse stayed sitting on the bed. Vera glanced at the door. She could probably just make it to that door and out of here, if she were quick. She took two rapid steps, but tripped over a jumper that was lying on the floor. The nurse caught her and made her sit down. She was looking at her in an odd way.

"Come on, we'll soon have you sorted. It's a bit of a tip in here. What have you been up to?"

"We haven't been up to anything."

Vera let her clean her hand. Perhaps it would shut her up and get rid of her.

"Don't tell me: it was Mr. Nobody again?"

She smiled at Vera, but Vera wasn't amused.

"I don't know what you think is so funny."

"Oh Mum, come on, I'm not saying anything's funny."

Vera snatched her hand away.

"And will you stop calling me 'Mum'. I am NOT your mum and have no wish to be, thank you very much."

The nurse reached out for her hand again and Vera slapped her across the cheek with it as hard as she could. The blow forced the nurse's head to the side. Vera got up quickly, watching fascinated as her handprint warmed up the pale face of the woman on her bed.

"Now, I'll thank you to get out of here."

Vera's voice was shaking, but she would not

tolerate strangers making fun of her and telling her what to do.

The nurse was standing too now, her hand covering the cheek, which Vera had slapped. Just a warning slap. That would teach her. Without saying a word, the nurse picked up her bag and left the room, slamming the door behind her. Vera waited to see if the door would open again. She crept closer to it and put her ear against the door. She heard sobbing on the other side. Something inside her felt wrong, felt crumbly, but she didn't understand why. She sat down on her bed and started to scratch her hand again. The smudges of red on her skirt grew larger.

24

My poem has magic powers

Katie

"Katie! Are you with us?"

Mrs. Jackson's voice was suddenly very loud. I looked up. She looked cross. I wondered how long she had been saying my name. I'd been doodling around my poem.

"I think we would all love to hear your poem now please, Katie."

I got up slowly and pushed back my chair before making my way to the front of the classroom, clutching my poem in my shaking hand. I was always scared anyway when I had to do something in front of the whole class, but this…well, this was like I was standing there and telling everyone my gran was a weirdo and Carys was a mean bully. She'd kind of slipped into my poem, like she deserved to be in it somehow. Suddenly the poem didn't seem like such a good idea, after all.

"Right then, Katie. Just take a deep breath

and off you go."

Mrs. Jackson was smiling encouragingly at me. All eyes were on me. I saw Carys smirking at me, but then I saw Molly and she gave me the thumbs-up. Even Anna grinned at me. She hadn't been with Carys at break time, she'd hung about near me and Molly until we asked if she wanted to play with us.

I decided that I was going to do this and I was going to amaze the class. I was sure it was a good poem. Who was Carys anyway? Just a girl who thought too much of herself. One day she was your friend and then she wasn't. True friends didn't do that and writing my poem had made me realise how angry she made me feel.

Being angry was definitely better than being scared or sad. In fact, writing the poem had made me realise how lots of things were making me angry. The more I stood there at the front of the class and thought about it, the more angry I felt, so that when Mrs. Jackson spoke, I was ready for her. I could almost feel Hugo by my side, wagging his tail. Weird.

"Katie? We could do with hearing your poem before lunch, not after it."

Mrs. Jackson was smiling at me, but it was one of those smiles that sits on top of something else and hers was sitting right on top of a pile of impatience. It didn't matter. I didn't care. I stood up straighter, raised my poem higher and took a deep breath.

"It's called, 'The Imposters.'"

I'd found that word in my thesaurus and loved it. You could say it by really spitting out the 'p' in 'poster' if you were cross.

"It all started when she moved in.
She says she is my gran.
The imposter."

(This time I spat out the 'p').

"She looks like Gran.
She wears her clothes,
but what gran leaves the house
wearing her pants outside her trousers?"

Most of the class laughed at that, although it wasn't strictly true. It was funnier than saying about her bra though and it went with the poem better.

"She's not Supergran.
She's Madgran."

Laughter again. It was going well. I raised my voice for the next bit, which I knew would make them laugh even more.

"She cooks her stockings in the oven.
She puts her teeth behind the cushion,
she shouts when she is cross,
she breaks things when she is sad.
She broke Mum's heart the other day.
She took my room and now
          there is no room for me.

I do love my gran.
I love the way she sings to Elvis,
I love her cheeky smile,
I love the way she blames Mr. Nobody
for everything that goes wrong.
But I miss my real gran and
now and then,
I see her in The Imposter's eyes
but not for long.
Gran has gone.
And in her place
it's not Supergran,
it's Madgran.

I'm living in my sister's room.
My bed is in the corner
but I have nowhere to go.
Nowhere to hide.
Nowhere to be alone.
Nowhere to be heard.

So I come to school and work
        and play and talk.
And I run. I run from home, I run from Gran.
I run from the room that isn't mine.
But now I'm running again.
I'm running from a friend who isn't a friend.
Who doesn't understand.
Who's mean and angry and cruel.
That's not how friends should be.
She's an imposter too."

The class was deadly quiet. I was sure they could all hear my heart thumping. I'd read that last bit without looking up from the page and I'd heard my voice getting louder and angrier, but it had all come out without me doing anything, like the words were pulling my voice out faster and louder, until the poem ended.

I wasn't scared any more. I had stood up and told them all how it felt to be me right now and I had showed them what a stupid fat idiot Carys had been. I looked right at her and she actually looked away. I felt fantastic. I was buzzing and wanted to run round in circles and pump my fists into the air. It was like my insides were bursting to get out, to cheer, to clap. I had told on her, but I hadn't said her name and she knew now, and so did everyone else. She couldn't hurt me now. My

176

poem had powers. It could protect me. I looked back down at it in my hands and it was like I could feel Hugo by my side again.

I had screwed up the edges of the poem in my excitement when I'd finished reading it, but it didn't matter. It was like my words had raced around the class as I had spoken, crowding round Carys until she was too embarrassed to look me in the eye. Mrs. Jackson was speaking, but I'd missed a bit, I think. The class was clapping so I made my way back to my seat. My cheeks were on fire. The rest of the lesson was a blur.

"Katie, could you just stay behind a moment, please?"

Surprised, I stayed where I was while everyone else filed out of the classroom, a few of them looking back at me curiously. I felt a bit nervous now. I slipped my hand into my pocket where I had put my poem, folded up into a neat little square. I had thought I would put it with my best pictures, but I was beginning to think I liked the feel of it in my pocket. It made me feel safe. It helped me not to be scared.

When the last person had left the classroom, Mrs. Jackson shut the door and came and sat down next to me. I turned the poem over in my pocket and kept my eyes on the table.

"That was a very moving poem you read to

us."

She paused like adults do when they want you to say something. I kept quiet.

"Mr. Braithwaite mentioned your gran was living with you. Did she move in this term?"

I nodded.

"The way you wrote your poem showed us all how hard it must be to get used to things being very different at home. Is there anything you want to talk to me about? Anything I can help with?"

She paused again and this time I couldn't have spoken even if I'd wanted to, in case I cried instead of speaking. I frowned hard and counted to ten inside my head, feeling the poem between my fingers.

"Katie, has there been some trouble at school?"

I didn't want her to get involved. I'd sorted it out now. It was going to be fine tomorrow. My poem had done it. I shrugged my shoulders.

"If there's something I can do, or someone I can speak to for you, then you must tell me."

She put her hand on my arm, which made me jump. I think I startled her too, because she pulled her hand away.

"You've been very quiet at school recently, a bit distracted. I wondered whether there was something wrong. Have you fallen out with someone?"

I was going to have to speak to make her stop. She should have done something about Carys before. I'd sorted it now, without her. I clutched my poem in my pocket as I spoke.

"It's fine."

I glanced up at her from under my hair. She was waiting.

"Really. It's OK now. I was upset but it's sorted out now."

She sort of pursed her lips like she didn't believe me, but she couldn't do anything if I didn't tell her anything.

"Well OK then, but you must come and talk to me if things are upsetting you that much. I love that you can write about it in a poem, but next time come and talk to me before it gets that bad. And if you change your mind, you know where I am."

She was smiling at me, but I desperately wanted to be out of there. I wanted to run. I wanted to run all the way home into the wind and run so fast that the wind would pick me up and carry me along, sending me higher and higher and further away until I could float on a cloud and into a dream. I picked up my bag and left.

Molly was waiting for me, because it was my day for going to her house, but I told her that I was going to Margaret's instead and my dad had arranged it all with her mum. Her mum would find out, but by then I'd be at Margaret's and all I wanted to do was run from school as fast as I could.

I couldn't speak when Margaret opened the door, I was panting so much. She looked surprised, but in a happy way.

"Hello you."

I was still panting, but I grinned at her and she stepped back so I could come in.

"What brings you round after school?"

I took a deep breath to try and stop panting.

"I did it!"

Margaret smiled, but she didn't understand.

"I mean, I did what you said. I thought about what makes me happy and confident and I thought of you and Hugo and I copied some of your painting onto my poem and when I read it out, it was like Hugo was at my side and it really worked."

I was out of breath again. Hugo was barking and jumping around me. Margaret got me to go into her lounge and sit down, but I was too excited to sit down so I kept bouncing around the room trying to tell her why I felt so good.

"I wrote a poem. We had to write one and read it out and I wrote about Gran and how weird she is and how it makes me feel. It makes me feel angry and sad and Carys is mean and I told them all how horrible she is and how she isn't really a friend, but I didn't use her name and everyone knows who I meant, apart from Mrs. Jackson. She doesn't know anything."

I felt like I might burst, or just shoot up to the ceiling and stay up there and zoom around like a firework rocket.

Margaret was laughing and Hugo was still barking.

"Katie, Katie! Calm down or you'll wear Hugo out. You've worn me out already."

"Sorry, but it was *so* cool. You should have seen her face and Anna isn't friends with her any more."

Margaret nodded.

"Well, I did speak to Anna's mum and explain what happened in the woods, so she may have had a word."

I flung my arms round Margaret and hugged her tight.

"You're the best!"

Then the doorbell rang. Margaret went out of the room to answer it. When she came back, she had Lou with her and a serious face on.

"Katie? Lou here tells me that you're supposed to be somewhere else right now."

Trust Lou to come and spoil my perfect day.

"Katie, Mum is freaking out. Molly's mum

rang our house and we'd just got back, so she made me come round to see if you were here. You're in BIG trouble."

I didn't want Margaret to be cross with me. I couldn't work out what she was thinking.

"Go on then, off you go. Next time, you need to let your mother know where you are, or at least ask before you come round. OK?"

I nodded. All my bounce had gone, like an empty balloon. Margaret smiled at me.

"Come on, don't be sad. It was lovely to see you and I'm so glad your poem went well. Just make sure you ask before you come round next time. Go on, off you go."

It was OK; she was still smiling at me. I gave Hugo a cuddle (he was hiding from Lou) and we left.

"What poem?"

I shrugged.

"Oh, just a poem about Gran."

"Can I read it?"

"No."

"Charming. You'll show it to some old woman, but not your own sister?"

"I didn't show it to her and she's not just 'some old woman' and anyway, it's none of your business."

I clenched my fist around it in my pocket. I don't know why, but I just didn't want to show her.

25

Aunt Sal comes round and is stupid again

Katie

Gran needed new teeth but she wouldn't go to the dentist. I didn't like going either, because the dentist always knew that I was still sucking my thumb. It was only at night, and not even every night, but no one else knew and every time we went, the dentist would ask me and I'd go red. Then Mum would tell me off for not stopping. I couldn't help it. It helped me sleep, but I never did it on sleepovers.

Gran needed to go, because her teeth kept slipping out when she was eating and if you were unlucky and sitting opposite, they'd fall into her gravy and splash you. Ugh. I think maybe it was because she kept taking them out and probably didn't put them back in properly. We were always hunting for Gran's teeth. Yesterday I found them in the biscuit tin. Imagine if Molly had come round and I'd offered her a biscuit and she'd reached in without looking and pulled out Gran's teeth. They were disgusting too, because she wouldn't clean them and wouldn't let Mum clean them for her either, and Mum had stopped having so many arguments with her about it now. And there was no way she'd let Dad near them.

I'd laid the table and put Aunt Sal opposite Gran so she could see what it was like when her teeth fell out. I'd helped Gran to some extra gravy just to make sure it was good when it happened. I'd decided I didn't like Aunt Sal; she'd upset Mum last time she was here.

"Well, Mum, you're looking well."

"Oh thank you dear, yes, can't complain."

The rest of us said nothing. I was praying for her teeth to fall out and splash Aunt Sal's yellow jumper.

"How are you feeling?"

"Oh, fine thank you. How are you?"

Gran was doing it again – having a normal conversation. She never had normal conversations with us. I didn't get it. Aunt Sal would never believe that Gran was weird. Gran's house had been sold and Mum and Dad had invited Aunt Sal over to discuss what to do with the money. I only knew that because I'd overheard them last night. That's all I heard because they'd shut the door just when it was getting interesting.

Gran's teeth started to make that clacking noise they make when they're about to fall. I felt Lou looking at me and I risked a look back and bit my lip so I wouldn't giggle. Lou was smirking. Gran put her finger in her mouth to push the teeth back into place and she almost managed it but then….Splash! Ace! Just enough reached Aunt Sal for her to pull a face.

She sat there, looking stunned as Mum went round to Gran and sorted her out. Mum gets all the worst jobs. Aunt Sal looked at Mum.

"Does that happen often?"

Mum nodded.

"Yes, I'm afraid it does."

"Oh these blasted teeth. I keep telling *her* that she must take me to the dentist."

Gran was staring hard at Mum and now Aunt Sal was too. Gran was unbelievable. Aunt Sal turned to Gran.

"I'm sure Lisa will take you to the dentist."

Gran smiled and shook her head.

"Oh no, you don't know what it's like here. *They* don't want to help you, you know."

Now Gran was staring at Dad. The air felt heavy again, like all the grown-ups' thoughts were waiting to explode. I shut my eyes and thought I could see Mr. Nobody waving a conductor's stick, keeping all the thoughts up in the air, waiting to choose which one would come down first. Actually that would make a cool picture. I jumped and opened my eyes quickly as Dad snapped first.

"Oh for goodness sake, Vera. Sal, this is what we have to put up with. If you came around more often, you might see that."

Dad got up and started crashing plates together as he cleared the table. We hadn't even finished eating yet. I held my breath. Even Lou was waiting.

"Well, I don't think that's fair on Mum or me. She's obviously distressed about her teeth, anyone can see that. I don't know why they haven't been sorted out, but there's no need for you to speak to her in that tone – or to me, for that matter."

"They haven't been sorted out, because she won't go to the dentist. We have tried, on numerous occasions, to take her but she will not go and unless you expect us to physically force her into the car, then I don't see what you want us to do."

Dad stormed out to the kitchen. Gran started scratching her hand. Mum wasn't eating any more. I had a sprout in my mouth but I couldn't swallow it and really needed to spit it out, but I didn't dare move. Lou was giving Aunt Sal the Look.

Aunt Sal seemed to remember I was there and smiled at me, though I thought she had a shaky voice when she spoke.

"Well Katie, this is all a bit heated isn't it?"

I glared at her.

"Listen girls, I think Dad and I need some time with Aunt Sal, so why don't you help clear the table and then make yourselves scarce for a while?"

Lou and I looked at each other and then Lou got up and started to pick plates up. I did the same. We took them out to the kitchen where we found Dad leaning against the worktop with his eyes shut. He opened them when we came in, but it was like he didn't see us for a moment, then he tried to smile.

"Thank you, you two. I'll do this, you just go upstairs, will you?"

"OK" said Lou.

That was very unlike Lou. I followed her out of the kitchen and up the stairs but when we got to the landing, Lou turned round and sat down, pulling her knees into her chest and then putting her finger to her mouth to tell me to be quiet. I sat down next to her. They weren't talking yet. Dad was still clearing up and I think Mum was putting on a movie for Gran to watch. She wouldn't watch it all, because she normally fell asleep after lunch anyway. Lou and I waited, side by side. It felt weird, in a nice kind of way. I didn't want to say anything in case I spoiled it. I sneaked a look at Lou. She looked kind of older and younger all at once. Older because she looked cross like Mum does sometimes, but younger because she was biting her nails and all huddled up. I didn't like the silence so I started to whisper.

"Aunt Sal's stupid, isn't she?"

"Well, she's definitely annoying. Yeah, whatever, you're right. She is stupid."

Lou never agreed with me.

"I mean, why doesn't she get that Gran is just weird?"

Lou looked at me and smiled.

"Yeah, she is pretty weird isn't she? But I guess Aunt Sal isn't here very often, so she doesn't see it."

"That's because she's dumb."

Lou smiled again, but it was a distracted adult smile. I wanted her to agree with me again.

"They shouldn't just give her away to a home though, should they?"

My tummy somersaulted as Lou gave me her 'How Stupid Are You' Look.

"She can't stay here. There's NO way she can

stay here any more. You don't know the half of it."

"What do you mean?"

How could she say that? I was always the one who could sort Gran out. I was at home more than Lou anyway, so I saw everything.

"It doesn't matter."

"What do you mean?"

"Never mind. Quiet! They're sitting down now."

"Tell me."

She hesitated, biting her nails again, and then she looked at me.

"Why not? You should know really. You know that mark Mum had on her face last week and she said she'd walked into the door?"

I nodded. Mum hadn't wanted to talk about that.

"Well, she didn't walk into the door. Gran did it. She hit her."

I stared at Lou. Why would Gran hit Mum? Lou raised her eyebrows at me and shrugged.

"It's true, but don't tell Mum I told you."

"But she can't have done."

"Well she did, alright. Now just shut up, I'm trying to listen."

I knew Gran was weird and annoying. She made Mum and Dad argue, she was scared of Dad and she accused them of stuff they didn't do.

She was embarrassing. I knew all of that, but she was still Gran. She sang Elvis songs and her old school playground songs and she laughed and she needed my help and…and yet she wasn't Gran, because sometimes Gran came back into her eyes and looked at me for just a few seconds and I knew she was there. But then it was like Mr. Nobody snatched her away and left us with this gran. Imposter Gran. The gran who'd hit her own daughter.

Mum had told Lou, but not me. Again. I shivered. Lou put her arm round me. One minute she was Nasty Lou then she was *Charlie and Lola* Lou, the nice big sister. I wish she'd just stick to one of them. I shuffled closer to Nice Lou. I must have missed the start of the conversation. I still couldn't believe that Gran would hit Mum. Aunt Sal was speaking.

"I understand it must be hard for you and I'm sorry I can't come and help out more. Really, I am, but you have to understand as well that because I'm not here, I'm not living through this so I need you to explain why exactly you think she's so bad she needs to go into a home. If it's just because you haven't got the time to look after her, then just say so. There might be other options. Maybe we could get carers in."

"Stupid cow, what does she know?"

Lou had taken her arm off my shoulders and

was hugging her knees again.

"Sal, it's not just about time. But you're right, we *don't* have the time to be full-time carers and that *is* what she needs."

That was Dad's careful voice, the one that's like a lid, that if you flick it off, the real angry voice will fly out from underneath. The air was heavy again; it was like I could feel Mr. Nobody sitting on my shoulders.

"Well then, I'm not trying to be difficult, but tell me why she needs full-time care."

She wasn't just being difficult, she was being dumb as well. Mum spoke next.

"She can't be trusted in the kitchen because she can't remember what she's doing. She gets confused and even though we have meals-on-wheels delivered, she still tries to make cups of tea and why shouldn't she? She puts the teabags in the kettle and yes, while that may be funny, one day she will turn the hob on again and forget about it and burn the house down."

There was silence again. I wish I could see their faces. Mum spoke again; she sounded fed up.

"She won't wash. She can't dress herself properly, she leaves the house without her coat and wanders off and gets lost. She turned up at Katie's school the other day and Katie had to bring her home. We had the school phoning up to check that everything was OK. It's not fair on Katie. She's only nine; she shouldn't have to deal with this."

Silence. I wish I could see Aunt Sal's face. I bet Dad's angry vein was throbbing. It sounded like it was.

"She hates me; she thinks I'm trying to kill her. She hit Lisa in the face, for God's sake. What else do you need us to tell you? It's got way past the point of us not having enough time to look after her. We can't *cope* with her any more *and* we can't give her the support that she needs. We need our lives back, our family back. And she needs professional full-time care."

I was crying and I couldn't stop. I wanted our family back too and now that Dad had said it out loud, I wanted it really badly. But I wanted Gran back the way she used to be, too. I couldn't stop the tears. Lou was holding me and trying to get me to be quiet, but it was no use, the tears kept on coming and coming and they were noisy, gulpy ones. I tried to stop, but I choked on the tears instead. I didn't want Lou to get angry with me for making a noise and I wanted Mum and Dad to come and comfort me. I wanted Aunt Sal to go away and I wanted the heavy feeling to go away too and the Mr. Nobody nightmares. All of it. I wanted all of it to stop.

I don't know what they agreed with Aunt

Sal, because they heard me crying and Mum came to find me. We went into her room and cuddled on her bed for ages until I fell asleep. When I woke up it was dark and Aunt Sal had gone home.

26

Carys gets into trouble

Katie

I was almost late for school today, because I couldn't find my shoes anywhere. It was Lou who suggested I look in Gran's room. Gran said she hadn't seen them, but she was actually wearing them. She wouldn't believe me when I said they were mine, so in the end I just asked if I could borrow them and she took them off and gave them to me. Sometimes it was best just to be in Gran's world, but I was still the only one who thought that.

I ran into school and was practically the last one into the cloakroom. I threw my coat onto my peg and stuffed my hat and gloves into my bag. My poem was still there at the bottom of my bag. It was my lucky charm. I took it out and pushed it into my trouser pocket. It was like I had Hugo by my side and Margaret smiling behind me as I pushed past Carys (who was standing by herself trying to look cool) and went into the classroom. I blanked her until morning break when I couldn't ignore her any more because she came up to me. I was in the playground, near the doors, waiting for Molly and Anna who'd both gone to the loo.

"Alright?"

I couldn't work out whether she was going to be mean or not, so I just shrugged at her. She took a step closer and I put my hand in my pocket and curled it around my poem. I didn't move, but I did turn away as if I'd found something more interesting to look at. My heart was whacking against my chest, like Hugo's tail against my legs.

"What're you doing then?"

She was so close, she was almost touching me. I turned my head to look at her then and something inside me just snapped. I pushed her away with both my hands shoving her in the chest. She stepped back but I could tell she was angry because she stood up taller. I'd had enough.

"I'm trying to avoid *you* actually. I've had enough of you. Everyone's had enough of you. Anna doesn't play with you any more and nor does anyone else. You're just horrible to everyone."

I could tell from her face that I'd upset her

and she was trying not to show it. She pushed me back against the wall, but I wasn't scared any more. How dare she?

"GET OFF ME!"

I pushed her off me and just at that moment Mrs. Jackson came out of the building. She looked mad angry.

"What on earth is going on here? Katie? Carys?"

She'd been followed out by Molly and Anna. Before I could reply, Molly spoke.

"It's Carys. She's a bully. She's always being mean to Katie and hitting her and shoving her and making fun of her."

"It's true. I was trying to get her off me. She pushed me against the wall."

Mrs. Jackson looked at Carys.

"Is this true, Carys?"

"She was being mean to *me*. She said nobody likes me."

"Yeah well, that's because you're mean and horrible to everyone."

I probably shouldn't have said that. Mrs. Jackson made us all come inside for a "chat." It all came out – how she'd thrown sticks at me and Molly in the woods, how she'd pushed me over, that she was always making fun of me and I told Mrs. Jackson that I'd meant Carys in my poem when I said about a friend who was mean. And

197

when Mrs. Jackson asked Carys what she had to say to all of that, she started crying.

"Is this all true, Carys?"

She nodded but she was still crying like *she* was the one who had been bullied.

"I think you need to say something to Katie, don't you?"

"I didn't mean to. It's just that everyone always makes a fuss of Katie."

"Carys, I'm waiting for an apology."

"Sorry."

She said it in the quietest voice possible.

"I'm going to have to call your parents, Carys. I will not tolerate this kind of behaviour in school. Do you understand?"

She was crying again. She'd started when Mrs. Jackson mentioned her parents. I almost felt sorry for her. I'd hate it if my parents had to come in, but Carys' parents argued about everything so they'd probably argue about this too and it would all be Carys' fault. She shouldn't have been mean to me, though.

"Right, the rest of you can go back out for what's left of break time. Carys, you and I need a chat."

Margaret and Hugo picked me up from school and this time Mum had arranged it with Margaret. Well, actually it had been Margaret's

198

suggestion and she'd said we could do some baking at hers when we got back. I hadn't really done any at home since that time I burnt the chocolate in the microwave. Gran was always wanting to help but getting stuff muddled up, getting in the way and she kept eating all the mix before we'd put it in the tins. It was just easier not to do any baking any more.

Hugo was *so* excited to see me. He rolled right over on top of my foot and waited for me to rub his tummy. He was so cute. He doesn't like strangers though, so when others from my class started crowding around us, he ran underneath Margaret's legs. She said he must have been very badly treated in the past and that's why he ended up at the rescue centre. I hoped people wouldn't think Gran had been badly treated when she went to the home, because she could tell them whatever she liked and they'd believe her.

Hugo ran ahead on the lead but kept coming back to see me and wagging his tail all the way home. It was such a cool day; I couldn't stop grinning.

"Good day at school?"

"Yep. Carys got into trouble for being mean to me."

"Oh, well that's good, isn't it? I thought that would happen soon."

"How did you know?"

"Oh, we just did, didn't we, Hugo?"

Margaret stopped to stroke Hugo's ears when he came back from sniffing at something in the hedge.

That was the thing about Margaret, she always seemed to just know stuff. I fingered the poem in my pocket.

"Margaret, do you believe in magic?"

"Oh now, there's a question."

"Well, do you?"

She was thinking, so I waited. Margaret always gave me a proper answer, not an adult 'made-up-to-please-you' answer.

"I believe that some things happen without us knowingly controlling them, but they happen because we just appear to be in the right place at the right time."

"So…does that mean that you *do* believe in magic?"

"Well, sometimes things happen when we want them to and we can't explain it, so yes, I think maybe I do."

She smiled at me, with her sparkly-eyed smile.

"I think getting Hugo was magic. I didn't know I needed him and he needed me but something drew me to the rescue centre that day – a story I'd read in the paper – and when I saw him, I just knew."

200

"I think meeting you was magic."

I was a bit embarrassed saying it, but it was true. It was great having Margaret to talk to and since she'd given me her picture, the bullying had stopped and I'd got braver. I just wished she could make Mr. Nobody go away now, or at least make Gran better so she could move back to her own house. Or a flat for old people because we'd sold her house.

"Well I think meeting you was magic, too. Now let's get back and make those chocolate brownies."

I think she misunderstood me. I didn't just mean it was brilliant that I'd met Margaret, I meant *real* magic. That evening I drew a new picture and stuck it on my pin board. It was Margaret the magician, with sparks flying out of her wand and Hugo at her side.

27

Vera prepares to defend herself

Vera

Go on, get one out and keep it.

Vera looked in the cutlery drawer. She needed to lay the table for Lisa and Sal for when they came home from school, but as she'd reached for the knives, she'd stopped.

What are you waiting for?

Pete was back, telling her what to do. Everyone was always telling her what to do.

He'll try to poison you again, you know. So will she.

She frowned. He was right; she didn't feel safe any more. Maybe she should keep·one close by. She took out a knife and held it up. She ran her finger down the sharp side. It wasn't very sharp. The doorbell rang. Flustered, she put it back and shut the drawer. Someone was coming in.

"Hello, my love."

"Hello?"

"Brought you a lovely beef casserole today, love."

"Oh. Oh, lovely thank you, but I didn't order one."

"Don't you worry about that, my love, it's all been ordered for you. Now let's get you a plate out, shall we? I see you've started laying the table."

Vera stood uncertainly as the stranger went into the kitchen and appeared to know exactly where everything was. She came back with a plate of food.

"There we go. Why don't you sit down?"

Vera did as she was told.

"Dearie me, you've forgotten a knife. Let me go and get you one."

The woman left and came back with a knife. Vera didn't like the look of the food. She pushed the plate away.

"There you are."

The woman placed a knife on the table in front of Vera.

"I don't want this muck."

"Oh it's not that bad, really it isn't."

The woman hovered. Vera picked up her

fork and pushed the food around her plate.

"That's it, my love. Right, off to my next one now. I'll see you again tomorrow."

And she left. Vera sat there, pushing the food around her plate with her thing, the whatsit that puts the food in her mouth. Its name was sitting there, playing hide-and-seek in her head. She pushed the food around more fiercely, cross with herself for forgetting the name of it, cross with that woman for leaving her with this brown steaming muck, cross with *him* for teasing her about *them*.

She picked up the plate and threw it across the room. It hit the wall with a satisfying smash and she watched as brown lumps of meat and gravy and mashed potato slid down the wall. She walked across the room and into the kitchen, deliberately treading on the shattered bits of plate and mushy food on her way. She took the knife that was in the sink waiting to be washed up and tested the edge of it across her thumb. She cried out as the sharp edge drew a line of red across her skin. The knife clattered to the floor and she bent down to pick it up.

That's it my love, now go and hide it somewhere safe.

28

Why does Lou know stuff I don't?

Katie

Lou was at a friend's and Dad was late home, so when Mum and I got home from school, it was just Gran in the house. When we got out of the car, our neighbour, Kevin, came out to see us and I instantly knew why. I could hear the telly from the pavement.

"I've been banging on your door, but I don't think your mother can hear."

He looked really annoyed.

"It's been like this for at least an hour."

Mum started fumbling for her keys.

"I'm so sorry. She gets confused. I'll switch it off."

He didn't even say thank you. Just stood there frowning, with his arms folded. He was retired. Dad said he didn't have anything to do with his time apart from find things to complain about. He was always complaining about where we parked our car, but this was the first time he'd complained about Gran. I'd seen him watching us through the curtains. I didn't like him. He never smiled. Anna said he was the grumpiest man on our street.

We got in and Mum went straight into the lounge and turned the telly off. I think that's why she didn't see the mess in the dining room. I was still staring at it when Mum came through.

"What on earth?"

Mum put her bag down and went closer to the wall. She had to be careful not to step in the mess on the floor. Somebody already had and there were footprints on the stairs' carpet.

"MUM?"

Mum shouted up the stairs.

"MUM? CAN YOU HEAR ME?"

I bet Kevin could. Mum ran upstairs and I followed. She opened Gran's door without knocking. Gran was shoving clothes into plastic bags.

"Mum! What are you doing?"

"This."

"Pardon?"

"I'm doing this. Can't you see?"

It would be bad to laugh now, Mum wasn't

in the mood.

"What are you doing with your clothes?"

Gran started to sing:

> "Down by the river,
> down by the sea,
> Johnny broke a bottle and
> blamed it on me.
> I told ma, ma told pa,
> Johnny got a spanking so
> ha, ha, ha."

It wasn't really time for singing either.

"Mum, do you know anything about the mess in the dining room?"

Gran looked at Mum really indignantly.

"I do not."

"The smashed plate? The food on the floor? The footprints on the carpet? Mum, what happened?"

Gran shook her head.

"Not me. Oh no, you're not blaming this one on me."

It was obvious it was Gran. It couldn't have been anyone else and anyway, there were brown marks on the carpet in my room, not poo like last time, but the same as the food on the wall downstairs. It made me feel funny inside that she'd actually picked up the plate and thrown it.

It was like Mr. Nobody was getting stronger. My real gran wouldn't do something like that. I looked more closely at her and something about the way her face looked so kind of pleased, but indignant at the same time, scared me. I didn't recognise her any more.

"Oh don't tell me, it was Mr. Nobody again, was it?"

"Yes."

Gran folded her arms. I mean I could understand why she didn't want to eat it, I wouldn't have done either. But I wouldn't have thrown my plate across the room.

"Oh, what's the use? Come on Katie, out of the way."

Mum waved at me to move, as she turned round to get out of Gran's room. It wasn't *my* fault; she didn't have to get cross with me. She pushed past me and thumped down the stairs, just like Lou does. I decided not to join her. Instead, I went upstairs. Lou was going to be late back so I knew exactly what I was going to do. I hadn't looked since that first time. I reached to the back of her bottom drawer and pulled out Lou's diary. Then I tipped the pen pot out to get the key and snuggled down under my duvet with the diary so if anyone came in, I could quickly hide it away.

I wanted to know what Lou thought about

Gran, and I wanted to know what was going on in Lou's head, because I couldn't work her out at the moment. No one was quite how they used to be. I guess I wasn't either. I mean, I'd never thought a poem might have magic powers before. I still wasn't really sure, but there was something about how it made me feel when I read it out and how I could actually *feel* Hugo by my side. And school was all sorted now, ever since that day.

I flicked through the pages. There weren't many to flick through since the last time I looked. I guess after she broke up with Max, there wasn't much soppy stuff left for her to write about. I couldn't find anything about me this time, which was annoying, but also good, I guess, because she wasn't moaning about me. She really wasn't being Lou. At last I found the entry I was looking for, dated just before Aunt Sal came round for Sunday lunch.

Thursday 5th December
Overheard mum and dad talking tonight. Apparently the real reason mum has a bruise on her face is because Gran hit her. Dad was furious and wanted to go and have it out with gran but mum stopped him. Said there was no point. I hate seeing mum like this, she's just so sad all the time and she's always tired. Dad's just cross. Gran hates him I think but we all hate her. I HATE her. She's ruining

209

everything and I wish she would just die and put
everyone out of their misery. It's all just a game to
Katie. She's always trying to prove she understands
Gran better than us but she has no clue. Sometimes I
envy her that she doesn't really get it. I looked at her
"secret" pictures yesterday. Well freaky. She's got a
thing about Mr. Nobody. He's in nearly every picture.
And that picture she got from the old wacky painter
woman is just creepy. It's no wonder Katie has
nightmares. See, gran has to go. Mum's miserable,
dad's just always cross, Katie's mental and that just
leaves me. I don't want to be a part of this and if she
dares hit mum again, I'll hit her back. Stupid old cow.

OK, so she was still Lou then, still being
mean about me. She'd never dare hit Gran
though, I knew she wouldn't. She was right
about Mum and Dad, but it wasn't just Dad who
was cross, Mum was too. Cross *and* miserable. It
was like Mum disappeared sometimes too, kind
of like Gran. I wondered if there was a place that
each of us went to when we weren't being the
real us. I hope it was a happy place, like a
swimming pool somewhere really hot.

Sunday 8ᵗʰ December
   Finally stupid Aunt Sal got the message. Gran
needs to go into a home. She's agreed to use the money
from gran's house to fund it. It was probably Katie's

*breakdown that did it. It shocked Aunt Sal, the stupid
cow. I don't see why we had to get her permission
anyway. We're the ones who are looking after her.*

I didn't have a 'breakdown' whatever that
was supposed to be. Just got really upset, that's
all, but if that sorted Aunt Sal out then that was
good. I think.

*There's a waiting list of course. Dad and I have
already been to see a few homes and mum and Aunt
Sal didn't know. We'd kept it quiet because dad had
said they'd be upset. I just don't get mum sometimes –
upset having gran here and upset if she goes. I mean
she hit her!!! Though I guess if I was mum and mum
was gran it would be weird having to put mum in a
home. Not as weird as having mum hit me and accuse
me of trying to kill her though. Mum just needs to get
over it. It's not as if gran is like she used to be and is
ever going to get better.*

She might get better. What did Lou know?
And why was Lou doing secret stuff with Dad
too? Why did nobody ever include me? Still, I'd
get my room back. And I'd get Mum back and
Dad too. I hoped I could get a new carpet. Mine
was disgusting now.

I felt kind of sad for Gran, though. She
wasn't going to like living with strangers. I

hoped they would be nice to her. I couldn't picture the home. I couldn't get the image of a rescue centre out of my head with grans in cosy rooms behind bars, like dogs in kennels. I hoped she could take her music with her. I don't think she could survive without Elvis. I think I'd miss her Elvis songs. I could get her a new collection for Christmas to take to the home with her. I wondered if she'd be there by Christmas. That would be nice, for us anyway. And Gran might get to play party games. She'd like that.

29

Vera finds Pete and loses him again

Vera

Vera was in an awkward position on her bedroom floor, trying to reach under the bed. He'd told her it was here somewhere, but now she was looking, she couldn't remember what she was supposed to be looking for, or indeed, who 'he' was who had told her to look for the thing. There was a lot of stuff under the bed, most of it plastic bags and clothes. Some of the clothes she thought she recognised, but some she was sure weren't hers. It annoyed her that people would come and put stuff under her bed. Probably those girls who lived here. She didn't get a good feeling from the taller one. Never smiled.

Vera heaved herself up by leaning on the bed. She must get on, she had things to do.

Go on then, off you go.

"I'll go when I'm ready, thank you very much."

No time like the present.

"Oh, just stop your pestering."

Vera turned round sharply, hoping to catch him unawares, but she turned into empty space. Gone again. A photo frame caught her eye, sitting on the table. A tall young man with long black hair, wearing a flowery yellow shirt and purple flared trousers grinned back at her. The grin tugged at her, pulling her towards the photo. She picked it up and stared at it, tracing Pete's features with her index finger, now numb and cracked at the tip. She couldn't feel him.

Come on, put me down.

Startled, she dropped the photo frame and put her hand to her mouth to cover the cry that escaped.

She stepped back from the photo on the floor, which was lying face down on the carpet. She backed away, trembling, until the backs of her legs found the bed behind her. She sank down heavily onto it, never taking her eyes off the photo frame. She felt the warmth of his arm across her shoulders and started to cry.

Hey now, don't cry. I'm here now, it's all OK.

She felt Pete hold her tighter and she let the tears run. The door opened and she didn't look up. Someone sat down on the other side of her and put their arm around her.

"Hey Mum, what's up? What's happened?"

Vera shook her arm off and stood up, looking wildly around the room, but all she could see was the woman on the bed.

"Where's he gone? What have you done with him?"

"What do you mean? Where's who gone?"

Oh no, she wasn't having this. How dare she pretend?

"You know full well who I mean."

The woman shook her head. Vera could feel her rage boiling up inside her chest.

"Pete! Where's Pete?"

The woman looked at her for a moment before replying.

"Do you mean Dad? Your husband, Pete? He's gone, Mum. Remember? He died two years ago. He had a heart attack."

She was standing now and holding out a hand towards her. Liar. Vera stepped backwards and felt the hard edge of something under her foot. She looked down and saw the photo frame. She bent down and picked it up. She looked at the woman who thought she knew it all. The woman who had taken away her Pete. Her fist clenched around the frame and she raised her hand as high as she could. Then she heard a bang and a voice coming up the stairs.

"MUM! I'M HOME. WHERE ARE YOU?"

The woman shouted back, still looking at her.

"I'm up here with Gran, Katie. I'll be down in a minute."

Vera recognised the voice that came up the stairs. Something inside her softened. She lowered her hand and turned the photo frame over so she could see his face. She traced over it with her index finger again, and again felt nothing. When she looked up, the woman had gone.

She was all alone.

30

Carys apologises

Katie

"Did she really mean it?"

"Yes, Lou, she really did."

"So that means that we can have Christmas all to ourselves? Really?"

Gran was going to Aunt Sal's for Christmas. We were all amazed. Dad was rubbing his hands together, grinning at us.

"Yes, really. So girls, we'll drop Gran off at Aunt Sal's on Christmas Eve, we'll come back and start the party, have a lovely Christmas all to ourselves and then she'll bring Gran home on Boxing Day and stay for lunch. It's all arranged."

He looked at Mum and smiled, a real smile that started on the inside. She smiled back. Lou rolled her eyes, but she was smiling too.

"What party, Dad?"

"Our family party, Lou. We'll have mince

217

pies to bake, paper chains to make. Christmas classics on the radio. Champagne for me and your mother. Maybe even a drop for you two, if you're good."

Dad loved Christmas. Well, we all did, but me and Dad especially. It was our job to get the tree and we were going to do it this afternoon. It always had to be as tall as Dad and he was tall – taller than my friends' dads so our tree was always massive.

Gran would probably enjoy herself at Aunt Sal's because she could play with the twins. They were nearly two, so they'd be really excited. I wasn't sure how Gran would cope somewhere new, though.

"Dad, do you think Gran will be OK? I mean, does Aunt Sal know how to look after her?"

"Well, she will learn Katie. It's only for a couple of days and I'm sure they'll all be fine. We might switch our phones off though, just in case."

He winked at Lou and Mum glared at him, though it was only a half glare.

"Would you really?"

"Probably not, no. I don't think your mum would let me."

"No, I wouldn't."

Mum put her arms round Dad's neck and kissed him right on the lips. Ugh. They used to do that a lot. The lounge door opened and Gran peered round it, looking at each of us in turn and then closing the door again. No one said anything but it was like she'd sucked Christmas out of the room when the door shut. Mum moved away from Dad and went to open the door. Dad seemed to shrink down like a giant had pushed a hand down on his head. He did a long deep sigh, but then looked at me and smiled again. A 'trying-hard' smile that started and stayed on the outside of his face.

"Come on, Katie. Let's go and get that tree. How big does it need to be?"

"Humungous!"

"Not big enough."

He was properly smiling now. It had reached his eyes.

"Colossal!"

"Done, let's go!"

We left Mum talking to Gran, and Lou doing stuff on her phone. I think she had a new boyfriend and wasn't saying. She was *always* on her phone. I was glad it was up to me and Dad to get the tree. Lou and Mum would be too distracted to get a good one.

We went to the garden centre just outside town. It had Christmas tree lights everywhere and Father Christmas and elf statues that moved.

There were those toy fairground things on fake snow, stockings, advent calendars, tinsel and sparkly stuff everywhere and there was Christmas music and real carol singers, if you got the right day. I loved it. I always wanted to buy something and Dad always said that it was sparkly tat, but he let me buy one new Christmas tree decoration every year. And every year we'd go to the café and have a drink and a cake. Today I had hot chocolate and a chocolate log. Dad had a cappuccino. He used to let me eat the froth off the top when I was little. I reached out with my spoon and nicked a bit off the top of his coffee. He pretended not to notice.

It was like it was all normal again and now Gran was going to be at Aunt Sal's for Christmas, it was going to be even better. Though I did feel kind of sorry for her. But not sorry enough to wish she wouldn't go.

We finished our drinks and went outside to look at the trees. I ran straight to the biggest ones. They had to be bushy *and* tall. I found the one I wanted but it was so big, I couldn't pull it out.

"Dad! I found one. This one!"

I was trying to yank it out as I called out to him, but he didn't answer so I let go and turned around to wave him over. I couldn't see him anywhere. Maybe he'd found another one. He wasn't on my row of trees, so I went round the other side and still couldn't see him. I looked down the next row of thinner trees, but he wasn't there either.

"DAD!"

Just when I was starting to panic, I saw a dog exactly like Hugo. I followed it for a bit through the rows of trees but he was too fast for me. I found Dad, though. He was standing next to Carys and her dad by the smaller trees and when he saw me, he waved me over. I didn't want to see Carys today. It was our special day, mine and Dad's, and not even Gran had ruined it yet. I walked slowly over to them.

"Come on, slowcoach. Apparently Carys has something she wants to say to you."

Carys looked at me and looked down at her feet. I frowned at Dad to try to tell him I didn't want to be here. I'd found us a tree and that's all we should be doing right now. He just raised his eyebrows at me and nodded his head towards Carys. She still wasn't looking at me, but I could see she was really embarrassed. She'd gone red, like I do.

Carys' dad looked at me and smiled like he was sorry about something and then he pushed Carys in the back, kind of towards me, but she tried to shake his hand off.

"Sorry."

She muttered it into her coat, but I heard her.

"Say it like you mean it and say it louder, Carys. We can't hear you."

Her dad was waiting with his arms folded.

I was embarrassed now. Carys looked up at me. There were tears in her eyes.

"Sorry."

"That's better, but still not good enough. Sorry for what?"

He smiled apologetically at my dad. Dad sort of smiled back, but mainly looked embarrassed too. I just wanted to go and get our tree so I tried to stop it.

"It's OK."

"Well that's very gracious of you Katie, but Mrs. Jackson's told me exactly what's been going on at school and I've told Carys precisely what I think of her behaviour. I'm glad we bumped into you and your father. I want to hear Carys say she's sorry properly to you."

Carys was trying not to cry now. She was doing those big sniffs. She looked at me and I tried to look back in a way that said it was OK, because even though she'd been mean and horrible, it was all sorted now and she'd never do it again. I knew she wouldn't.

"Sorry I was mean. I didn't mean to be."

She wiped her gloves across her face and looked up at her dad. He nodded at her and then held out his hand to shake my dad's. Weird. I looked at Carys and rolled my eyes at her. She did a tiny smile back. We'd be OK. Dad and I left them looking at the tiny trees and I took Dad's hand and led him to the biggest one that I'd found.

"This one."

"Looks great."

Dad pulled it out and examined it.

"So, why didn't you tell us about Carys?"

I bent down, pretending to straighten out some of the lower branches.

"There was nothing to tell."

Dad pulled the tree away from me and started dragging it over to where they put the net around it.

"Well, her dad was very apologetic when he saw me. I gather he had to go into school to talk about her behaviour, and from what I understood, it was all to do with bullying you."

We were standing in the queue for the net thing. I shrugged.

"Well, she *was* mean, but I sorted it."

"How did you sort it?"

I couldn't really tell him about my magic poem, could I? And if I told him that I'd talked to Margaret about it, then he might get upset that I hadn't talked to him about it.

"I told Mrs. Jackson and she told Carys off."

That was true, really. Dad helped to push our

tree into the net machine.

"Well, next time there's any bother at school, you need to tell us. We can't help if we don't know, can we? Had it been going on for long?"

I nodded and slipped my hand into Dad's as we waited for the tree to come out the other end. Dad squeezed my hand and then he let go and helped the garden centre person swing our tree onto a trolley. It was all wrapped up now, like a caterpillar in a cocoon. We didn't say anything else about Carys and I was glad because I wanted to feel Christmassy again. It was nice that Dad knew, though.

We had to push the tree into the back of the car through the window and have it sticking out of the side of the car like we do every year. It was the only way to get it home.

We carried our tree up to the front door and walked straight into an argument.

31

Gran loses it

Katie

"I know what you're up to."

"Mum, we are not *up* to anything. Whatever you think is going on here, it isn't."

I'd opened the door and Dad was behind me. The tree was outside, because Dad needed to trim its bottom before we brought it inside. The voices were coming from the kitchen. I stayed where I was and started taking off my hat and gloves. It had been freezing driving home with the back window open.

"Just you keep away from me. I'll scream. I will. Don't you think I won't."

I wished she'd gone to Aunt Sal's already. Dad hung his coat up and went straight into the dining room with his boots still on. I took mine off and hovered. I wanted to know what was going on, but there wasn't room for me in there.

Gran always seemed to think someone was up to something. She raised her voice.

"Get him away from me. He's evil."

The lounge door opened and Lou appeared. She looked at me and I shrugged. I'd only just got back, I didn't know what it was all about. We stood by the door and watched as Gran picked up a knife from the chopping board, where Mum must have been chopping vegetables, ready for lunch.

"Mum, put that down."

Mum moved towards Gran and held out her hand. Gran held the knife in front of her. Her hand was shaking. I heard Lou gasp next to me. I felt sick.

"Don't you come near me. I know your game."

"Lisa, stay where you are. Vera, please, just put that knife down. You don't need it."

She had her back against the worktop and Mum was in front of her. Dad was now standing next to Mum. He towered over Gran. She looked up at him and waved the knife in his direction.

"You'd like that, wouldn't you?"

"Yes, Vera, I would. Please put that down."

I didn't understand.

"Gran!"

Her head turned to look for me.

"Gran! It's me, Katie. What are you doing?"

She looked at me like she didn't understand either and in that moment she seemed to lower the knife a bit. Mum tried to grab her hand but then it all happened too quickly. I just saw a flash of metal as Mum cried out and the knife fell on the floor. Mum was doubled over, clutching her hand and Dad was shouting.

"You stupid woman! What have you done?"

He picked up the knife, I think, and Gran shrank away from him. Mum was standing up again, but still holding her hand and blood was dripping onto the floor. I felt dizzy. Lou pushed past me and pulled out a chair for Mum who sat down on it. Lou yelled at me.

"Katie! Get Mum's work bag."

But I couldn't, because I felt dizzy and sick and my legs were wobbly and wouldn't work. Then everything went black.

32

Vera is scared

Vera

"When I was just a little girl
I asked my mother what will I be?
Will I be pretty?
Will I be rich?
Here's what she said to me:
Que sera, sera,
whatever will be, will be.
The future's not ours to see,
que sera, sera."

Vera sang the song to herself quietly as she moved around her bedroom, opening doors and drawers and picking things up and putting them on the bed. She felt that the song should comfort her, like it used to when her mother sang it to her. But her mother was gone now. Everyone was gone now and she was being kept here and the people here were angry. They didn't like her and she didn't feel safe.

She knew The Thing had happened but she couldn't picture The Thing, didn't know what it was, but she knew it was bad. She didn't know who had done it, but she didn't like it. And Pete was quiet. She'd asked him what was going on, but he wouldn't answer her. Something bad though, she knew it was something very bad.

She looked down at the back of her hand. It was red raw and bleeding again. It did that when there was something bad. It hurt. She found something to wind around it to make it feel better, but she couldn't finish it, do the thingy that would hold it together, that thing that took the ends and tied them together. Brown Owl knew. Brown Owl had taught her when she was a little girl at Brownies. She'd be cross with her for forgetting. Everyone was cross with her now.

33

I tell Margaret what I want to happen

Katie

We hadn't done the tree yet. It was still in the front garden. I'd fainted, Mum said. She made me sit on the sofa with my feet up, drinking water. I'd only ever fainted once and that was when Lou had slammed her finger shut in the door and the nail went all yucky.

Dad had bandaged Mum's hand where Gran had cut her with the knife. I'm sure Gran hadn't meant to. I think I might have confused her when I shouted to her, but Mum said it wasn't my fault and she wasn't badly hurt so there was no damage done. Dad didn't say anything. The vein in his forehead was throbbing. He left Mum and me on the sofa and went outside to start chopping off the bottom of the Christmas tree.

Gran was in her room, like she'd been naughty and sent to bed. Lou had gone out. "Just out," she'd said when Mum asked her where to, and Mum didn't even bother trying to argue with her. Told her to be back by five. I thought I would go out too.

"Mum, I want to go out."

"Oh, well I can't take you anywhere this afternoon, can I? Besides, I thought you were going to help Dad with the tree?"

"Not really in the mood now."

I rested my head on Mum's shoulder and picked at my cuff. It was my favourite blue jumper and it was getting frayed at the edges.

"Oh Katie, come on. Don't let this silliness put you off."

I moved away slightly to look up at her face. She was smiling at me but her face was tired. I didn't think she looked very well.

"It's not silliness, Mum. Gran stabbed you."

"She didn't stab me. It was an accident; I startled her. My fault really."

She looked at the carpet as she said it. It wasn't her fault.

"Can I go out? Please?"

Mum leaned her head back on the sofa and shut her eyes.

"Well, where would you go?"

"I'll go to Margaret's. I'll ring her first to

check she's in."

Mum kept her eyes shut.

"OK, but you can tell Dad he's got no one to help him put the tree up."

I rang Margaret and I told Dad and they were both OK with it. Dad said he'd get it put up and put the lights on and leave the decorations until I was back. Margaret said she'd baked some German Christmas biscuits and I could help her eat them.

I just wanted to get out of the house. I didn't like the way it felt. It was like this morning had never happened and no one was excited about Christmas at all any more. Gran had done that, or Mr. Nobody anyway. Both of them, together and they'd taken away my special Christmassy time with Dad, just like they'd taken away my room. And if that knife had gone any deeper or had got Mum in her tummy or somewhere else in her body, then they might have taken my mum away too. I wished they'd go now. That's what I told Margaret too.

"Oh, I'm sure you don't mean that."

Margaret had black coffee and I had hot chocolate and Hugo had a chew stick treat. We had a plate of biscuits each. They were spicy and she said they were traditional German biscuits, called Lebkuchen. She must miss her family in Germany.

"I do. Gran's ruining everything. I can't believe she stabbed Mum."

"I'm sure it was an accident. Your poor mother. Does she need anything?"

I shook my head and tickled Hugo under his chin.

"She just needs Gran to go away, but she keeps defending her."

"Well, it must be hard. It is her mother after all. Just think how you would feel in her shoes."

I couldn't. My mum wasn't mental.

"Aunt Sal's having her for Christmas but I wish she would have her now."

Then a horrible thought came to me. What if she couldn't go to Aunt Sal's because she was too dangerous? Aunt Sal wouldn't want her if she thought she might stab the twins. I felt Hugo licking my hand. He must have wanted to cheer me up, or maybe he could taste the biscuits on my hand. I buried my face in his fur. I wished I had a dog. He'd be better than a gran.

"It'll be OK. I'm sure your mum and dad will sort it out."

I wasn't so sure. They hadn't managed to so far, had they?

"I just wish she'd go."

I said it to Hugo but Margaret heard me.

"I know you do. It'll be OK, you'll see."

I didn't see how she could be so sure. We did

some painting before I went home. It was the first time Margaret had let me use her paints. I painted my room, back the way I wanted it to be, with all my stuff in it again (but I left Gran's telly in it). I left it at Margaret's house to dry. That was her idea; she said she'd drop it off the next day.

34

Vera runs away

Vera

The man was bringing in a tree and he'd left the door open. Vera watched him from the bottom of the stairs. She'd put a few things in a thingy that you put things in. Really, it was hopeless that she couldn't remember its name. She couldn't stay here. It wasn't safe for her any more. Something had happened that made it not safe. He was badgering her though and she didn't like it.

"Just leave me alone. I'll go when I'm ready."

She hissed it fiercely into the air, knowing he could hear.

Do it now. The door is open. Now's your chance.

"I know, I know. Just be quiet."

He was right behind her on the stairs but she wasn't going to turn and look, she had to concentrate. The door was still open, the man was in the other room with the tree and there didn't appear to be anyone else around. Vera walked quietly and quickly to the door, clutching her handbag and the…bag! That was it – bag. Of course!

She stepped outside into the chill air. Luckily she'd put some layers on to save her packing everything so she was well wrapped up against the cold. She set off down the street, with him chipping away at her heels.

Come on! Faster! You need to get away!

She mumbled under her breath to him to be quiet, keeping her head down and her eyes focused on her feet. She didn't want to trip. There was a small crowd of people at the bottom of the hill, waiting. She waited with them and crossed the road when they did. When they got to the other side, she followed, but a little way behind, as she couldn't keep up with their young legs.

No spring chicken now, are you, my love?

Vera chuckled, feeling free as a leaf in the wind. She started to sing.

"I shouldn't have gone away,
so I'm walking back today.
Walking back to happiness with
you-oo-ooo-oo."

She turned around to share her happiness with Pete, but he was gone. There was no one there. He'd said he would come with her. He said that they would be together until the end. She stood facing into the icy wind, feeling it wrap itself around her, while she searched for her beloved Pete and strained to hear his voice, but there was nobody there.

Vera turned back round as a group of teenagers jostled around her, laughing, shouting to each other, and moving on. She held her bags closer to her and followed in their wake. She wasn't sure where she was supposed to be going but better forwards than backwards. She kept going until her feet hurt, along the High Street, past shops with words in windows that she couldn't decipher, with snowflakes and trees and sparkling lights, shoppers busily going in and out, laden down with bags. People bought too much these days. She wanted to tell them that, but they rushed around too fast for her.

Pete would have warned her about interfering in other people's lives. She'd wanted to warn Lisa about marrying that man of hers. She didn't like him. She couldn't really say why, just didn't. Pete did though. Pete said he was just right for Lisa. Two lovely kids they had, but she hadn't seen them for a while. She stopped, trying to remember when the last time had been. They felt familiar to her, yet far away.

Stopping had caused someone to bump into

her and because she was tired, she supposed, she'd fallen. And it hurt. She was aware that it hurt and that she couldn't move and someone was bending over her. And suddenly there was an awful lot of fuss.

35

Gran goes missing

Katie

When I got back from Margaret's, Mum was stressed. Gran was missing. Apparently she'd slipped out when Dad was bringing the tree in. He was out in the car looking for her now, but they didn't know how long she'd been gone, so they didn't know how far she might have got either. The thing is, Gran did go out sometimes and most times, somebody who knew us or her brought her back. So it wasn't such a big deal.

"She's emptied her handbag."

I looked at Mum and waited. I mean, that was odd, but so what?

"She's left her purse at home and that's the only thing she's got with any ID, so if she gets lost, no one will know where she lives, and she won't be able to tell them."

"Oh."

That *was* bad because Gran *always* got lost. That was why Mum and Dad didn't like her going out by herself.

"I think she's packed some clothes. I can only think she packed some in her handbag. Her room is littered with clothes."

Gran did have a large handbag. A *Tardis*, Dad called it.

"Shouldn't you have gone out to look, instead of Dad? I mean she doesn't like Dad, does she? She might not come home with him."

Mum frowned, as if I'd said something sensible. Which I had.

"No, I have to stay here in case someone calls or she comes back."

So we stayed at home. Lou wasn't back yet and Dad had rung to say that he was going to go up to the woods to have a look. I pretended to watch the telly but I wasn't really. I was thinking about the picture I'd painted of my room and how I'd wished that Gran wasn't in it any more. And now she wasn't and my picture was at Margaret's. She knew I wanted Gran to go and she'd said everything would be OK. She'd said that about Carys and Anna too, and then they'd stopped bullying me.

I went upstairs to get my poem, which was in my school bag, and I sat on my bed and smoothed it out in front of me. It did look a bit like Margaret's picture on my wall. I shut my eyes and pictured Margaret in my head, with her curly white hair and huge smile, in her purple combats and purple matching woolly jumper. I felt safe with Margaret. If she had done anything to make Gran go, it had only been to protect me. Even thinking about her made me feel better and I could almost feel Hugo wagging his tail. It was like I could reach down and rub his tummy he felt so real, right there next to me. Maybe if I just spoke to Hugo in my head, he could help me to find Gran.

I didn't want her to get lost. I just wanted her to move out.

36

Vera's in hospital

Vera

Vera was in a bed and she hurt. Her head hurt and so did her arm. She couldn't move it. She tried to move her head but she couldn't really move that either. There was noise, but not noise she recognised. Voices, clattering, swishing, banging, murmurs. It reminded her of something, but she wasn't sure what. She tried to remember what she was doing here, but it was all too fuzzy and the more she tried to think, the more her head hurt. Her mouth was dry and she wanted a drink. She couldn't move her arm; she couldn't reach the cup she thought she could see beside her. She didn't have her glasses on, so she wasn't sure it was a cup. She tried to speak, but the words wouldn't come out.

Tired, she let her eyes close.

37

I need to find Gran

Katie

Lou was home now and Mum was still stressed. Dad hadn't found Gran yet.

I was drawing. I didn't think, I just drew. I let my pencil find the lines it wanted. I'd been thinking about Hugo, so I suppose it was no surprise that he was the first thing I drew. He was standing next to me and I was bending down and stroking him. I coloured him in black and decided to draw a cartoon strip. I drew Margaret next, in her studio. She was looking at a picture. It was my picture of my room. Then there was Gran and Mr. Nobody. He was dragging her somewhere. Mum looking stressed. Dad in his car. Lou with her hands on her hips. A shop window with Christmas decorations. Me and Lou holding hands.

I stopped drawing. Gran had gone to the

shops. I just knew it. Lou and I had to find her. I went to get Lou. She was sitting with Mum in the dining room. Mum was on the phone to someone, asking if they'd keep an eye out for Gran.

"Lou, we should go and look."

I was pulling on my boots at the same time as talking, so I couldn't see if Lou was giving me one of her Looks.

"Why you and me?"

I stood up and looked at her. I didn't have time to argue; I just knew we had to go. Gran needed us.

"Because I think she went to the shops, I can't go by myself, Mum wants to stay here in case she comes back or someone calls, and Dad's out looking in the woods. We have to go."

I went and grabbed my coat off the hook and zipped it up. Got my hat and gloves too. I was all ready and Lou had only just stood up. Mum was still on the phone.

I waved my arm at Lou.

"Come *on*."

She tapped Mum on the shoulder but Mum frowned at her. Lou looked back at me and nodded.

"OK."

She got her stuff on and by then Mum had got off the phone and come out to find us.

"What are you two up to?"

Luckily Lou answered so I didn't have to explain anything about drawings or Hugo and just knowing that we had to go. She wouldn't have believed me, I knew she wouldn't. I already had the front door open.

"We're going to check out the High Street. She might be in a shop somewhere, or someone might have taken pity on her and bought her a cup of tea or something. I've got my phone, I'll call you if we find her."

Mum nodded.

"OK. Make sure you do. Call me anyway in half an hour so I know where you are."

"OK" we said together.

I grabbed Lou's hand and pulled her out of the house.

"Hey! Don't."

She tugged her hand away and glared at me.

"Well, come *on* then. The shops will shut soon."

"Why are you so keen? She's probably just sat on a bench somewhere, or she's stabbed someone and is at the police station."

I hadn't thought of that. I stopped and looked at Lou, but she grinned at me.

"Got ya!"

"But she might have done."

"Nah. She wouldn't. She's only got it in for

Mum and Dad and me."

"That's not true."

"Yeah it is. You're the Golden Girl, even if she can't remember who you are. At least she likes you."

And that was why *I* had to find her. She liked me, she had no one else and I'd been wishing her away. I didn't want it to be my fault that she'd gone, even if I didn't want her to live with us any more.

We reached the High Street and I didn't know where to start. Which shops would Gran like? Lou led me into the curtain shop. She wasn't going to be in there, but I went in anyway. There wasn't much to see and we left. Lou shrugged at me.

"I thought she'd like the colours in the windows. Those curtains are like the ones she had at home."

Lou was full of surprises. I didn't think she really knew Gran, but maybe I was wrong. It was busy and the pavement was crowded with Christmas shoppers. I was beginning to think we'd never find her. I was too hot in my hat and gloves and wanted to stop and pull them off, but Lou was ahead of me, waving at me to catch up and I didn't want to lose her. There was a lump in my throat. This was all my fault. If I hadn't shouted, Gran wouldn't have looked at me, Mum wouldn't have tried to grab the knife and Gran wouldn't have cut her. She'd probably run away because she was scared and I bet that Mr. Nobody had persuaded her to run. Or maybe Margaret and Hugo had wished her away for me. Gran couldn't fight back against all three of them.

I caught up with Lou. She put her arm around me.

"Hey, come on. This was your idea."

I couldn't speak. The lump in my throat wouldn't let me.

"Come on, let's go into *Alfie's*. She might be having a cup of tea. We could ask someone if they've seen a batty old woman. I bet they'd remember."

We went in and now I was even hotter. Lou held my hand and pushed through the queue to the woman at the till. People were complaining about us. I could hear them. I thought I might cry. Lou must have asked the woman about Gran. I hadn't heard, because all I could hear was the voices of everyone we had pushed past, saying nasty stuff about us. I wanted to tell them we weren't rude, that we had an important thing to do, but it was too noisy and they were too unfriendly looking.

The woman behind the till shouted into the kitchen behind her.

"Gladys! Gladys!"

A woman with very red cheeks came out, wiping her forehead with a tea towel. Ugh. Sweat in the food. I wasn't going to come here for a snack.

"What is it?"

"Has there been an old woman in here, confused, maybe dressed funny? This girl here says her grandma's gone missing."

Gladys shook her head and looked directly at Lou.

"No, sorry love, not that I've seen."

"OK, thanks."

We started to work our way out of the queue, only this time I was in front and I had to do the pushing. I wanted to have a better look round, to see for myself if Gran was there. A woman put her hand on my shoulder to stop me.

"Excuse me, love. Did you say you were looking for your gran?"

My heart beat faster.

"Yes."

"Well, this may not be her, but there was an old lady earlier who looked like she'd had some kind of fall. An ambulance came. Do you know what your gran was wearing?"

I wasn't sure, but again, Lou surprised me by knowing more about Gran just then than I did.

"She was wearing black trousers and a green coat and she had a bright blue handbag."

The woman nodded.

"Well, I do seem to remember the handbag, so it might be your gran. Your best bet is to ring the hospital and find out if she's been admitted."

It must be Gran. I could feel it. But what if she was badly hurt? I asked the woman.

"Was it bad? The woman you saw – how bad was it?"

"Oh, I'm sorry love, I couldn't tell, but it was bad enough for the ambulance to be there. Don't worry yet though, it might not be your gran."

It was. I knew it. We got out of the café and Lou called Mum on her mobile and told her what the woman had said. I had a bad feeling about it. The air was pressing down on me again and making it hard to breathe. By the time we got home, I was soaked in sweat and my head felt full. I pulled everything off so I was just in my jeans and T-shirt and I collapsed onto the sofa. When I shut my eyes I saw *his* eyes, hundreds of them, staring back at me. Mr. Nobody had multiplied.

Mum called the hospital and they did have an old woman who'd come in but they didn't know her name. They described her and Mum said it sounded like Gran. She had concussion and a broken arm.

38

We visit the Home

Katie

We were at The Home.

It was a specialist Alzheimer's home, one of only two in the county. Dad had explained that Gran had been acting so weirdly, because she had this Alzheimer's thing. It was like a disease that ate away bits of your brain, so none of what she'd done was really her fault. It didn't seem fair that we should send her away for something that wasn't her fault. Maybe that's why Mum had waited so long before agreeing to find a nursing home.

It wasn't as bad as I thought it would be. We were there because Mum had rung up and explained about Gran and asked if we could come and look again. She was already on their waiting list. So the woman in charge had given us a tour. It did smell a bit, but Lou said that old people did smell, so there was nothing wrong with that. She's just rude. It's not the old people, it's the food they make them eat and all that cleaning stuff they use, mixed in with old flowers and clothes and maybe a bit of an old people smell. Kind of sprout-like. With elderflowers and lilies.

They all had their own rooms and they could bring their own curtains if they wanted. There was a telly lounge and a quiet lounge and a room for doing stuff like singing or games. There was a dining room and a conservatory and carpet and wallpaper and pictures on the walls. It was like a grand house really, with a lovely large garden. I thought Gran would like it.

We were in the conservatory when Dad asked about the waiting list and that was when Mum Lost It. The woman had just explained that they still had quite a long waiting list because they only had 12 places, and obviously they could only give someone new a place when someone else had died. Gran was supposed to be coming out of hospital in a few days, so that meant we needed someone to die soon. Dad didn't want her coming back to ours. I wasn't sure what Mum wanted. I didn't think we should be wanting someone to die, though. Gran was going to have to come back to ours.

Then Mum started to cry.

The woman noticed first. She just put her arms around her. She was a big woman so she kind of wrapped Mum up in her arms and Mum stayed there and she shook and shook and the woman just held her. Dad and Lou and I stood and watched. The woman led her to a chair and Mum sat down with Dad perched on the arm, his arm around her shoulders now. I was glad. He should be hugging her, not a stranger, even if she was nice. The woman was kneeling down on the floor next to Mum, who was still crying. A nurse came in with one of the old people, but the woman waved her away. Then she noticed us.

"Why don't you two girls go out into the garden?"

We both shook our heads and amazingly, no one said we had to. The woman turned back to Mum and gave her a tissue. Lou went and sat down near Mum but I stayed where I was, near the door. I'd never seen Mum cry like that. I felt the tears running down my face and I turned away from them all, so no one could see. I sat down on the floor behind a chair, hugged my knees into my chest and listened.

"It's hard, isn't it?"

I heard Mum blow her nose, a really long, snotty blow.

"Why don't you tell me what's happened recently?"

So she did. She told her everything, even the bit about the knife which I thought was stupid, because I wouldn't want Gran in the home if I was the woman, in case Gran stabbed her. But it was like Mum couldn't stop talking.

She told her that Gran kept accusing her of trying to kill her, that she wouldn't wash, that she smashed things against the wall, that she was scared to leave her in the house by herself, that she didn't feel safe any more and that she worried about me and Lou. The woman just let her talk and when Mum had finished talking, she cried and cried and I thought she would never stop.

It made me start crying too and I couldn't stop either. I didn't want anyone to hear me, but they must have done, because Lou found me and she sat down next to me and hugged me. When I looked up, I saw that she was crying too.

39

Lou is fab

Katie

Dad said it was all the crying that did it. Gran had been bumped to the top of the waiting list and the day Gran was due to come out of hospital, the home had rung us and said they had a "vacancy", which Gran could have. When Dad said "vacancy", Lou mouthed "death" at me and smirked. I thought it was sad, not funny.

Gran was going to go straight from the hospital to the home and Mum was going to take her by herself. It was the last day of term, so Dad couldn't be there and they wouldn't let us miss school, though I did ask. It was stupid. We'd only be making Christmas decorations or something. We never did anything important on the last day.

So while Mum was taking Gran to the home, I had to make stupid Christmas cards at school. It was a waste of time. I wanted to be with Mum. I didn't want her to start crying again without any of us there.

I was worried about Gran too, that she wouldn't understand what was happening to her. Mum said she was just going to pretend it was a little holiday. I didn't think she should lie, but I didn't say anything. She'd been stressed all week, so I was trying to be invisible. A bit like Mr. Nobody really, but nicer, obviously.

Since Gran had been in hospital, the house felt better, lighter, as if it was free again. When I walked around, I couldn't feel Mr. Nobody any more. I realised that he must have always been there when Gran was there, and he'd made everything feel smaller, darker and heavier somehow. I wanted to skip around the house and actually did, until Mum told me off for making too much noise. It was happy noise, but I stopped anyway, because Dad had told us we had to be extra helpful. Even Lou was being helpful. In fact, she was being so helpful she came to pick me up from school, because she finished earlier on the last day of term than me.

She was standing at the gate, trying to look cool, pretending she wasn't looking for me, even though I knew she was. So I tried to look cool too and when she saw me, I just nodded at her. I was walking with Molly and holding a card she'd made me. Carys and Anna were behind us. We were sort of friends now, but not very close friends.

Lou nodded at the card I was holding.

"What's that?"

I showed her.

"It's a card. Molly made it for me in class today. Do you like it? Look, it says, Happy New Room!"

Lou pulled a face, like she didn't get it.

"It's because I can have my room back now. That means you can have yours back, too."

"Oh."

She looked like she didn't care, but that was probably because she was still trying to look cool. Then I saw her Look, the one with her head on one side and her lips a bit pouty with eyes that screamed out: "LOSER!" But she wasn't looking at me. I turned round to see who she was looking at. Carys had deep red patches on her cheeks and was trying not to look at either of us. This was ace. Lou was giving Carys a Look for me. *Me!* I wanted to enjoy this.

"Bye, Carys. See you soon."

She ignored me and tried to walk past us, but Lou actually stopped her. Unlike me, Lou was tall and she easily held Carys back by the shoulders. She put her face really close to Carys', like Carys did to me. Her voice sent a shiver right through me. I wouldn't have liked to be at the end of it.

"Don't you EVER mess with my sister again, do you get it?"

Dad must have told her what happened at the garden centre, because I hadn't said anything. Carys didn't look at her, but she nodded and tried to pull away. Lou held on.

"I mean it."

Then she let go, looked at me and smiled.

"Right sis, let's go. You and me are in charge of making Mum's favourite tea."

We didn't make Mum's favourite tea because that was a Chinese takeaway. We baked a cake instead and we cleared up. It was nice finally having a proper big sister.

When Mum got home, she just walked up to Dad and they hugged. They didn't say a word, which was fine because I wanted to show Mum the cake.

"Look Mum! Lou and me made you a cake. It's chocolate. Shall we have some now? Dad says he's going to get a takeaway, so we could have a bit while we wait. Can we? Do you like it?"

Dad released Mum from their hug and she came to see our cake. I think it stopped her from crying. She pulled out a chair, sat down and pulled me towards her.

"Come here, you."

I did and I sat on her lap and she gave me a cuddle that squeezed my breath out of me, so I had to wriggle away. She was laughing. A sort of sad-happy laugh.

"Katie Franks, I love you."

"I love you too, Mum."

"You too Lou, come here. I love you both so, so much."

Lou came over and Mum put her arm around her too. I looked up at Dad.

"What about Dad?"

He laughed, and his laugh had tears in it too.

"I'm here. Family hug."

And he tried to wrap his arms round all of us, but of course he couldn't quite manage it. It was nice though. Back to how it should be. I shut my eyes and was sure I could feel Hugo's tail wagging against my leg.

40

Vera finds Pete

Vera

Vera felt a little strange, a bit woolly. Too much wine at lunchtime, perhaps. Just a glass she'd had. They'd said it was a special treat for Christmas Eve. She would have had more, but they hadn't offered it. They'd been very jolly about it with their Santa hats on, but they had taken the wine away. Maybe they would offer more on Christmas Day. It was a good dinner. She'd sent her compliments to the chef. She wondered when she was supposed to be going home. She might stay a bit longer, although the company wasn't great.

She looked around the room at the old people sitting near her. She'd tried to talk to the one next to her, the old man with the smart waistcoat, but as she'd said to Pete, he wasn't quite right in the head. That woman opposite, whose name she couldn't remember, was singing now. She recognised the tune and started to join in.

"Now there are three steps to Heaven.
Just listen and you will plainly see.
And as things travel on,
and things do go wrong,
just follow steps one, two and three.
Step one, you find the girl you love.
Step two, she falls in love with you.
Step three, you kiss and hold her tightly.
Now that sure seems like Heaven to me."

Vera closed her eyes and hummed along, feeling Pete squeeze her hand as he hummed along too. Somebody else started to sing and the tune changed but Vera stayed as she was with her eyes shut because sometimes, when she opened them, Pete was gone. And just now, she could feel him beside her, and that's all she wanted.

41

The best thing happens

Katie

I had another surprise before Christmas. It was Christmas Eve and I was at Molly's house for the day. We helped her dad do loads of baking. Mince pies, sausage rolls, chocolate fairy cakes. Her mum had to work until 4pm and that was when Dad was coming to pick me up. Molly's dad said I could take some of the baking back to my house.

I helped Molly wrap her Christmas presents up too. Christmas had been kind of forgotten in our house, apart from the tree. We'd all been too busy sorting Gran out. But today, Dad said that when I was at Molly's, he would sort my room out for me so I could be in it for tonight. I did want my room back, but I was a bit scared too, in case it didn't want me back. It didn't smell like mine any more and it didn't look like mine. I'd miss Lou too. I liked that she was there when I woke up from a nightmare. She was a lot better at being a big sister now.

I'd already wrapped my presents up. I'd got Lou a new holder for her phone. Dad had some comedy socks with the Simpsons on them and Mum a woolly hat, but the best present was one I'd made at Margaret's house. I'd drawn a picture of the four of us standing in front of a Christmas tree and painted a border of flowers around it all. Margaret had made a frame for me. I'd drawn in each of their presents, so that Lou was holding her phone in its new case, Dad was wearing his socks pulled up to his knees and Mum had her hat on. Margaret had said that that I should draw what I wished I could have, because she said dreams did come true sometimes. So I drew a dog that looked like Hugo, but I made a flap to put over the top of it, so that if I didn't get a dog, I could stick the flap down and no one would know that I didn't get what I really wanted.

I hadn't said what I wanted for Christmas. I hadn't even written a Christmas list and left it under the tree. But it was still going to be the best Christmas ever, because it was just us four. We were all going to visit Gran in the home on Boxing Day, but Christmas Day was just for us.

Dad was in a brilliant mood when he picked me up. His eyes were shining and he was really grinning, a proper one that started right inside him.

"Good day, Dad?"

"Shouldn't I be the one asking you that?"

"Yeah well, I can tell you're excited about something. What is it?"

Dad tapped his nose.

"Oh, just you wait and see."

"Dad!"

"No, you'll have to wait."

It only took five minutes to drive from Molly's house to ours and when we got home I raced inside. Mum and Lou were hanging around in the hallway. I pulled my boots off, flung my coat on the floor and raced upstairs. It had to be my room.

I threw the door open and stepped inside *my* room. *Everything* was back. My duvet cover, my stuff in the bookcase, my cuddlies on the bed, *all* the stuff that I'd packed away in boxes, my beanbag, my pictures on the walls and a brand new stripy rug on the floor. I walked right inside and looked all around. Mum, Dad and Lou were standing outside my door. Mum came in and I threw my arms around her.

"Do you like it?"

"I *love* it."

I loved that everything was back as it used to be and there was a rug to cover up the brown bits

263

on the carpet. It was mine and it was ace. Though I would have to change some of the pictures and some of the cuddlies could go back in the box. I was older now. It was a shame the telly had gone, though.

"Lou helped, you know. Told us where you'd want things."

She smiled at me, a *Charlie and Lola* smile. I gave her a hug too.

"I love it. Thanks Lou."

"'S OK."

The doorbell rang. Dad went to answer it and Mum and Lou followed him. I wanted to stay in my room and just feel it again. I sat on my bed and shut my eyes. It was perfect, so perfect I could feel Hugo's tail wagging against my leg. Then I heard him barking. Weird. I opened my eyes and gasped because he was actually here and he was going mad for me. I bent down and rubbed his neck and chest. He flopped over onto his side, waiting for me to rub his tummy with his paws in the air, one of them on my leg, with his tail wagging and wagging. Then I heard Margaret and looked up as she came into my room.

"He's happy to see you."

"I thought you were flying to Germany?"

Margaret had told me that she was spending Christmas with her daughter and family. She came and sat down next to me and then Mum, Dad and Lou crowded into my room, too. Hugo was still demanding tummy rubs.

"I am, but I'm flying out early tomorrow, and well, actually I'm staying out there."

She paused and I looked up at her. I didn't get it.

"What do you mean? For ever?"

"Well, yes, I suppose so. I'll come back and visit though and you're very welcome to come and visit me. My daughter has asked me to live with them permanently. They have a big house, she needs help looking after her children and I miss them. They even have a shed in the garden I can turn into a mini art studio."

I thought carefully before I replied.

"Do they have a spare room or will your grandchildren have to share?"

Everyone apart from Margaret laughed, which I thought was mean, because it wasn't meant to be funny.

"Not only do they have a spare room, they have a spare bedroom, bathroom and sitting room. I'll have my own little flat in their house."

"Really?"

She nodded.

"But there is a catch. They don't like dogs and I've been thinking anyway that Hugo needs to be with a family. He needs a family to grow up with him. So…"

I held my breath. I didn't dare say anything, in case I'd got it wrong. I looked at her and then at Mum and Dad. They were looking at each other and smiling. It must be true.

"Your mum and dad and I have been talking, and we would all like you to have Hugo."

I couldn't believe it.

"Really? But won't you miss him?"

"Yes, of course I will. I'll miss him a lot, but I know that you love him. Look at him: he loves you, too. I can't take care of him; I can't run around with him like you can. He'll be very happy with you."

"Oh, Margaret, thank you!"

I hugged her and then I jumped up and hugged Mum, then Dad.

"Thank you!"

Hugo was jumping around and barking, like he knew something exciting was happening too. Awesome!

The End

If you liked this book...

Getting published is really hard. Everyone told me that and I believed them, but I still hoped that I would persuade an agent to take my book on and find me a publisher. Then I was long listed in The Times/Chicken House Children's Fiction Competition 2014. I was sure, that with those magical words on my cover letter, an agent would pick my manuscript out of the slush pile and call me. It didn't happen, so I decided to self-publish.

If you enjoyed reading **Mr. Nobody**, please write me a review on Amazon. It all helps to make my book more visible to others. I don't have the might of a publishing house behind me, but I do have my readers and that's what should count the most. Thank you.

If you are curious to find out more about me, please visit my website:

www.nataliegordon.co.uk

Acknowledgements

Many thanks to fellow students and staff from the Lancaster University Creative Writing MA, who helped this book to emerge; in particular, thank you to Professor Graham Mort and Professor Paul Farley for their feedback on early drafts. The rest of the gang, you know who you are, and I'd especially like to thank Janet Lees and Isobel Staniland for their support, encouragement and feedback on later drafts.

Huge thanks to Dr. Becky Finkel, Rachel Ainsworth, Beth Gordon, Geoffrey Robinson, Tanya and Megan Bascombe for their brilliant feedback and suggestions, especially Tanya for those detailed proofreading observations.

Thanks to Clare Clayton for her fantastic cover illustration.

Thanks to Barry Cunningham and The Times/Chicken House Children's Fiction Competition 2014 for giving me the confidence to get this book out there.

Thanks to Millie and Isla Gordon for being my biggest supporters and to Millie especially, for being my first reader.

Finally, thanks to Adrian, for everything.

31141503R00162

Printed in Great Britain
by Amazon